Graveyard OF MEMORIES

WHAT HAPPENS WHEN THE MONSTERS IN YOUR MIND BECOME THE REALITY YOU FEAR?

ALEXANDRA REED

Cover Art by Book Cover by Design

Editing & Formatting by Gray Publishing Services

CONTENTS

Visit Alexandra Reed's website for the latest news and updates.

Website: alexandrareedauthor.wordpress.com
Twitter: @alexreedauthor
Facebook: www.facebook.com/darkandtwistyforever
Instagram: @alexandrareedauthor

DEDICATION

This book is dedicated to the memory of my beautiful mom—
my guardian angel and my hero. An amazing woman who was, is,
and always will be my ship in the storm.

ACKNOWLEDGEMENTS

I would like to give special thanks to my friends who have supported me on my journey through life and inspire me each and every day; Agata, Rich, Rachael, Emma, Jessie, Ali, Jessica, Romy, Helen, Sadie, Emma, Laura, Steph, and Jessika—thank you all for everything you do. Words will never express how much it means.

I'd also like to give Stephen, Ollie and Humphrey from Blake a mention for inspiring and motivating me through their amazing music. Your voices helped carry me through my darkest days and into the light.

A huge thanks goes out to my colleagues for putting up with me all these years.

Last, but by no means least, I need to give a special shout out to Kellie Dennis of Book Cover by Design for the wonderful cover design. Jimmy Thomas of Romance Novel Covers for the amazing artwork and for being the image of Drew/Tyson.

To my angel, the fabulous Tiffany Lynne of Gray Publishing Services, thank you for helping me to shape this lump of coal into a dazzling diamond.

Words can never express just how grateful and thankful I am to all of you!

Graveyard
OF MEMORIES

Screams reverberated through the night as people ran, hiding, trying to fight their way to safety. They—the ones who were infected, ceased to communicate weeks ago. Now all that remained were the echoes of voices from the past.

NEW AMERICA- 2025

Tyson Hawkins was stuffing what few belongings he had into a backpack when suddenly, he heard scratching and snarling outside his door. Reaching for his baseball bat, he flung open the bedroom door. Unfortunately, what awaited him wasn't anything he'd ever expected to see in his lifetime.

For a split second, he imagined he was in Hell. It was only when his recently deceased sister lurched towards him, grunting and drooling blood, that he realized this was Hell on Earth. Before he could react, she stopped, swaying momentarily, and finally collapsing into a bloody heap at his feet. Blood, shards of bone and brain matter were splattered all over him. Sickened, Tyson turned away—dry heaves wracking his body. Lifting his gaze, he found his brother—face pale, holding a bloodied hammer with shaky hands while standing over their sister's lifeless body. When their eyes met, he realized in that moment that life would never be the same again.

"What did you do?" he asked, his hands moving to cover his mouth.

Drew said nothing. The hammer continued dangling in the air as if in a symphony, and he was the conductor.

"What did you do?" Tyson repeated, taking a step back.

Drew shrugged at his younger brother, pain etched across his face. "What I had to do," he finally stated flatly.

Letting the hammer fall to the carpet, Drew stumbled back against the wall, grateful for the support it provided.

Without another word spoken, Tyson fell to his knees, closed his eyes and, for the first time in years, he prayed.

FOUR WEEKS LATER-TENNESSEE

Tyson was lost. He'd become separated from his brother in the chaos and, consequently, found himself alone and running out of gas. Instinctively continuing to head for the mountains, Tyson hoped that if he could get as far up as possible, he might stand a chance of surviving—for one night at least. He was just about to give up such hope when he came across a cabin. It was well hidden, just above what looked to be a row of smaller cabins, possibly one of the many hunting lodges that were scattered about the mountains.

Apprehension filled him as he cut the engine of his motorbike. Grabbing his gear, he cautiously approached the darkened cabin. Pressing his ear to the door, he listened. No sounds came from inside; no signs that anyone still lived on the premises. *This could be a good thing*, he thought. Drawing his knife, he carefully reached for the door.

Tyson inhaled sharply before carefully breaking one of the small windows in the cabin door. Quickly clearing the glass, he slipped his arm through the opening to quickly unlock the door. The last thing he wanted to do was break the door down when it could provide a necessary buffer between him and what lie in the darkness beyond. Locating the lock on the door, he turned it till he heard a familiar click. Breathing a sigh of relief, he entered the cabin and turned to lock the door behind him. He was about to explore his new sanctuary when he suddenly felt something sharp press into his neck.

"Who the hell are you and what do think you're doing breaking into my home?" A woman's voice hissed, pressing what could only be a knife harder into his flesh.

"Whoa there, honey, easy now," Tyson said softly, raising his hands into the air. "I'm sorry, I was just looking for a safe place to rest my head for the night. Figured the place was abandoned."

"You figured wrong," she snapped, the knife steady against his skin.

"Yeah, sorry. Guess I should've knocked."

"Uh huh," she replied. "Well, regardless, you're going to sit next to the door until the police show up."

When the woman mentioned the police showing up to rescue her, Tyson couldn't help but laugh. All the events of the last few weeks came flooding back to him, especially the part about becoming separated from his brother, the only family he had left. Now this woman was threatening him with the police. Considering the phones hadn't worked in weeks, it wouldn't make a whit of difference who she phoned.

What is she thinking? Or is she a little slow in the head? Despite the knife at his neck, his legs were far too tired to hold his large frame any longer, and his heart was too weary to care if she killed him or not. Slipping to the floor, more out of exhaustion than due to her threat, he reached out for support. The fact that he connected with a bare and shapely leg didn't escape his notice, nor did the fact that it sent blood rushing to certain parts of his anatomy. He gazed up at her, unable to see her clearly in the darkness.

"Let me go. Now," the woman ordered, a hint of fear in her voice.

"Sorry," Tyson muttered as he released her leg. Shaking his head, his shaggy, unkempt hair fell across his eyes as he tried to clear it. He was tired...so tired. *Now is not the time to think about screwing the first female I've come across in days,* he silently chastised.

"Lady, you know damn well you're not calling anyone, and the police sure as hell aren't coming. What are you playing at? Or do you not understand what's going on out there?"

The woman went quiet. Too quiet. Reaching out for the small flashlight on his belt, he flicked it on. She blinked, shielding her eyes as the beam of light landed upon her, briefly colliding with the light from her own.

As his eyes began to focus Tyson found himself staring at the most beautiful woman he'd ever seen. One he never thought he'd see again. *Damn it.*

He swallowed hard. "It's been too long, Violet."

Tyson averted his eyes as a flashlight was quickly aimed at him, "Ty Hawkins?" Violet gasped. "How the hell did you find me?"

"Don't take this the wrong way, darlin', but I wasn't exactly looking for you," Tyson retorted. Calmly reaching out to direct her flashlight out of his eyes, he continued. "How long have you been holed up here?"

"A couple of years now. Ever since—" she trailed off.

He was well aware of the reason she had run out on him; it was still a sore subject for him. And from the sounds of it, it was for her too.

Violet continued, "I heard something on the radio a while back about an illness spreading…strange things happening, but I haven't had a signal up here for weeks. I—um, don't get out much."

Tyson sighed, running a hand through his hair in frustration. *Violet apparently didn't have a clue—not a single fucking clue.*

"You really don't know what's been happening, do you?"

She looked at him, her head cocked to one side, brow furrowed. "And just what exactly am I supposed to know? Besides, why would I believe anything you have to say? Give me one good reason why I shouldn't kick you out on your ass right now?"

"Because your life may depend upon what I have to say" Tyson said, with quiet emphasis.

S tumbling through the woods, dry leaves crunched underfoot. A new day was dawning. Light was beginning to sparkle through the trees, chasing the shadows away. *If only it could chase away the monsters. If only they vanished with the darkness. If only*—There were far too many of those racing through her mind to even begin to fathom.

Kate Reilly leaned against the tree, trying to catch her breath. Glancing back, she could see that they were gaining on her. *Damn it. Either those things are getting faster, or I'm getting slower. Either way, I'll be dead if I don't find somewhere to hole up, and quick.*

Unfortunately for her, a life of studying and endless hours in her laboratory hadn't prepared her for this. Then again, no one had been prepared for this.

She gasped as a cold hand grazed her arm. It was as if death itself tried to get a grip on her. Glancing to her side, Kate could see that the corpse was fresh. Long blonde hair, matted with mud and blood, framed a petite face. Her eyes were glazed over as she attempted to feast on Kate. Struggling, Kate slammed its head repeatedly, almost effortlessly, against the tree. The sickening sound of bone crunching turned her stomach as the woman's head caved in and the corpse went ragged. Letting the body fall to the ground, she quickly scanned her surroundings. There were more, so many more, approaching from the direction she had come.

Increasing her pace, Kate set off, trying desperately to ignore the screaming of her lungs. She couldn't give in to it, not now. Choking back her fear, she pushed forward. In the distance, she could see a clearing in the trees, and what she hoped was the main road. Hearing them on her heels gave her all the motivation she needed to keep going. Digging deep, she somehow found the energy to make it to the road.

Momentarily blinded by the sun glancing off the metal of the abandoned cars, she allowed her eyes to adjust. Focusing on the road, she looked for something...anything to help her escape. That's when she heard the engine. Spinning around, she spotted a motorcycle approaching. For the first time in a long time, she allowed herself to cling to hope—like early morning frost.

Kate knew that her options were limited, but she would rather take a chance on the living than the dead right now. Moving to flag the motorcyclist down, she hoped and prayed that the person would stop. She had never hitchhiked before; it was something she couldn't do—she couldn't just give someone else control over her fate. Kate was always in control, had always been in control, but now, she felt as though she had been thrown into the deep end of a bottomless pool. Control was something she didn't have anymore, and it was extremely unsettling.

The motorcycle stopped an inch away, bringing her face to face with the most ruggedly handsome man she had ever laid her eyes upon. Her heart skipped a beat, and her breath caught in her throat.

"You want a ride or not, sweetheart? I ain't got all day," he growled, glancing over his shoulder at the swarm of undead weaving their way out of the woods. *Who knows how many more lie within the darkness of the forest?*

"Ye—yeah," she stammered. Grabbing hold of his shoulders, Kate hoisted herself onto the back of the motorcycle and held on as he revved the engine. Without another word, the bike shot off, leaving the corpses in its wake. Kate didn't look back—she knew that looking back could cost you your life, in more ways than one. If she were to stop and think of all she had lost, she may as well have thrown herself to the wolves. She bit back a laugh. *If only everyone knew what was really out there.* The things she knew...well, it would be enough to scare the toughest of soldiers, never mind the average Joe's running for their lives. Shaking her head, Kate forced herself to focus on the present and the reason she was in this predicament. She was the only one left—the only one who knew the truth.

It seemed an eternity before they pulled to a stop outside a row of buildings, the setting sun casting shadows over them. If they didn't hunker down for the night, those shadows could be the death of them.

"This is our stop," the stranger rasped, indicating she should get off the motorcycle.

Kate dismounted and stepped to one side, surveying her surroundings. The buildings were old, but seemed sturdy enough from the outside. Before she could say anything, he grabbed her arm, pulling her with him toward one of the doors. Forcing the nearest one open, he pushed her into the building. She watched as the man did a quick sweep of the rooms and then proceeded to secure the entrance for the night.

"What the hell were you doing?" he snarled. "Trying to get yourself killed?"

Kate stared at him as he towered over her, his large frame hugely imposing in the small room.

"I worked at the Medical Research Laboratory just outside of town. You know, one of those classified government facilities? After everything went to hell, I holed up there for a while until I ran out of supplies," Kate explained as she sank down against the wall, the coolness of the concrete seeping through her clothes. "I've been on my own for a long time, just trying to find somewhere safe to go. You're the first person who's stopped to help me."

"What are you, a doctor of some sort?" he asked, grabbing his backpack and settling down across from her.

"Yeah, you could say that," she laughed, wryly. "I'm Kate, by the way. Kate Reilly.

"Drew Hawkins," he said with a nod.

"Nice to meet you." Kate smiled.

"So, Doc, where are you headed? Anyone you can go to?"

"No, I don't have anyone. Nowhere to go either," she replied, her eyes betraying her pain.

Kate felt his eyes upon her. She shifted nervously, uncomfortable from being under such intense scrutiny. That was one of the reasons she had always hidden behind her lab coat and thick-rimmed glasses. It was easier that way. Or at least, it had been. Now, she was naked and vulnerable, in a world she knew nothing about, with a man who seemed to set her loins on fire with just one glance in her direction.

DREW

Drew couldn't take his eyes off her. She was the most beautiful woman he'd come across in…well—ever. She was also one of the most foolish—running around on her own, with no weapons or supplies that he could see. In his case, beautiful women usually meant trouble, and he sensed that this one was no different. And yet, the way she looked at him, he knew he wouldn't be able to walk away from her. He had debated whether to stop for her, but there was no way he could leave an innocent woman to fend for herself.

He just couldn't do it, no matter how much the world had changed. It was against his nature to turn his back on anyone who needed help, much less a scared and defenseless woman.

Kate cleared her throat, "Are you on your own, Drew?"

"No. I have a group in the next town. I was heading back when I ran into you," he said as he rummaged in his rucksack. Pulling out a bottle of water, he took a sip and handed the bottle to Kate.

"Why risk going so far on your own?" she asked, taking the bottle, and gratefully savoring the soothing liquid as she took a large swig.

Drew draped his arms over his knees. "A few weeks ago, my brother got separated from us. I've been looking for him ever since."

He blamed himself for not keeping track of Tyson, but it all happened so quickly. The corpses had caught them off guard. Tyson had managed to get a few of the survivors to safety, but he'd been cut off when he'd tried to return to help Drew and the others. The last time he'd seen Tyson, a swarm was chasing him. Drew had no choice but to get the rest of them out of there and find somewhere safer to hole up. He'd made a huge mistake in letting his guard down, and it was a mistake he wasn't about to make again. He was going to find his brother, and he was going to do everything in his power to not lose anyone else on his watch.

He knew the chances of finding his brother were slim, but these days you had to have the strength to hold onto hope. Without it, you risked becoming an empty shell of the person you once were. Drew wasn't sure if anyone else understood that feeling. *How exactly does one prepare for the loss of a loved one in times like these? Times when you only had to step foot beyond the safety of a wall or door and you risked getting ripped to pieces. How could you not hope for survival, for rescue, for life?* He wondered to himself.

Glancing at Kate, he realized she'd become lost in her thoughts too.

"Where'd you go?" Drew asked quietly, startling her.

"Sorry, I drift off sometimes. My own little world," Kate laughed dryly.

"Who did you lose?" he asked knowingly.

His question seemed to hit her like a punch to the gut. She inhaled sharply, a panicked look on her face.

"My daughter," she croaked, biting back the tears.

3

Shawn

"This place might still have some supplies," James Sullivan said. "Pull over here."

The street is quiet—too quiet, Shawn Robertson noted as the old pickup truck came to a stop outside a small shopping mall. Graffiti covered the walls and the glass panes were splattered with bloodstains as well as other debris.

Putting the truck into park, Shawn reached for his gun. "We'll be lucky if we can find anything a few weeks from now, Sully," he said, exiting the vehicle and bracing himself against the reek of death that would inevitably flood his senses.

"We're gonna have to move eventually—once things have dried up here," Sully replied, slipping a backpack on. Tucking his straggly, dirty-blond hair underneath his baseball cap, he pulled his hunting knife from his belt. "Remember, no shooting unless you have to, Shawn."

"Yeah," Shawn replied, his brow furrowed. "The quicker we get outta here the better, man."

They moved quickly towards the entrance, carefully stepping around the mutilated corpses strewn across the sidewalk, staying alert to any noises or movement.

Shawn entered the building first, stepping through the broken plate glass door, the shards crunching noisily beneath his hiking boots. He paused briefly before signaling Sully to follow. Together, they advanced silently into the darkness of the deserted mall. It didn't take them long to find what they were looking for, but from what they could see, there wasn't much hope of finding supplies here.

"You check it out, Shawn. I'll head down a bit further and scope out the other stores," Sully whispered, walking away.

"We shouldn't split up," Shawn hissed. "Sully? Dammit!"

Sully turned, giving Shawn a cocky smile and a-thumbs up, before continuing down the corridor. Shawn sighed. Slipping his gun into its holster, he carefully pulled out his knife instead. Regardless of Sully's cavalier attitude towards safety, he was right about using knives instead of guns. They certainly didn't need to draw any unwanted attention, at least—no more than they usually did.

Flicking on his flashlight, Shawn slowly swept the beam of light from side to side. There were overturned shelves and decomposing bodies littering the aisles. Making his way further into the store, he gagged when the stench hit him, briefly reminding him of a backed-up sewer. Pressing the back of his hand to his nose, he continued forward. No matter how many times he'd seen dead and mutilated bodies on the job, none of his police training had prepared him for this. Continuing to move forward, he carefully scooped cans of food into his backpack as he went. Turning the corner, his light settled on a shelf filled with bottled water.

"Bingo," he silently cheered

His joy was short lived, however, when shadows began to lunge at him and hands clawed at his jacket. Spinning around he found himself up close and personal with two undead corpses. Instinct suddenly kicked in. Shoving one away, he brought his knife up as he grasped the other by the neck and rammed the knife through the side of its skull. It struggled with him briefly before the blade sank into its brain, severing what was left of its miserable existence. Yanking the knife free, he let the corpse fall to the ground. Not wasting any time, he was on the other one before it could even get up, repeatedly stabbing it through its oozing eye socket, the rotting flesh making slurping sounds every time he removed the blade.

Shawn sprang to his feet, sweeping the flashlight around frantically, expecting more to be coming at him. After a few moments, with no sign of any other deadly visitors, he slid the knife back into his belt and began once again loading the water into his bag. As he was making his way out of the store Shawn found a few other essentials: more knives, batteries and some much-needed medical supplies. Hurriedly leaving the store, he returned to the pickup truck to load it before going in search of his wayward friend.

SULLY

Sully silently ventured deeper into the mall, darting glances into the various store windows, not seeing much of value. The further he went, the darker it became. That's when he saw *it.*

Stopping, he took in the sights of the greeting card store, all decked out for Valentine's Day. Balloon hearts and giant teddy bears graced the storefront, along with blood splatter and rotting bodies. It was a disturbing contradiction of life, yet it had little effect on him. He couldn't think about her, not yet. It was easier to just shut down and focus on getting through this daily hell they now called life.

The sudden sound of muffled screams snapped him from his reverie. Caution be damned, Sully darted towards the cries for help. The commotion was coming from a nearby bookstore. As he neared he could see a faint light emanating from within the store where he could hear men's voices jeering and taunting while a woman helplessly sobbed.

Pulling his gun, he momentarily considered getting Shawn until the woman screamed again. Throwing caution to the wind, he carefully stepped forward, rapidly assessing the situation. Four men in various stages of undress were standing over a young, blonde woman. Her clothes were torn and she was tied, spread-eagle to a desk. A red haze enveloped him. Aiming his gun, he fired in rapid succession, taking three of the men down before the gun jammed.

Seeing his comrades falling around him, the remaining man yelled, charging at Sully with a knife. Sully quickly ducked out of the way, but not before the blade could graze his upper arm. Swinging around, he kicked his attacker's legs out from under him before throwing himself on top of the large man. Sully, having the advantage, poised the knife over his heart.

Grabbing Sully's wrist, the man desperately tried to force the knife aside, but Sully was stronger. Anger fuelling his strength, Sully forced the knife down into the man's chest, pushing it all the way to the hilt, before twisting as he yanked it free. Relishing in the man's screams of pain, the blade came down repeatedly, inflicting more pain, blood soaking them both. It wasn't long before the man's screams became gurgles, blood trickling from his mouth. Sully watched at the life drained from the man's eyes, his body going limp.

Pushing himself to his feet, he kicked the man's body for good measure. Knowing that the gunshots could have attracted unwanted attention, he rushed to the woman's side, cut her bonds free, and helped her to her feet.

"Are you okay, ma'am?" he asked quietly, handing her the shirt that was tied round his waist.

"Y–y—yes, I think so. Thank you," she mumbled, gratefully slipping it on.

Sully watched as she tried to button it with trembling fingers. Pushing her hands aside, he deftly buttoned the shirt for her while quickly introducing himself. "I'm James Sullivan, but everyone calls me Sully."

"Julie...Jackson," she whispered hoarsely, wrapping her arms around herself.

"Come on, Julie, we better get outta here while we still can."

Just as Sully turned, heading for the exit, a bullet struck him, tearing through his upper arm. Pain seared through him, leaving him lightheaded. Falling to his knees, he heard Julie scream just before the sound of another shot rang out.

Crumpling to the floor at Julie's feet, Sully swore he heard someone calling his name through the distant fog that clouded his mind, bogging down his tired body. Darkness closed in, enveloping him in a warm, welcoming blanket of nothingness.

4

Violet

The graveness in Tyson's voice unsettled Violet.

"I think I'm going to need a drink," she said as she guided her flashlight towards the kitchen. Realizing Tyson wasn't following her she paused at the door. "You coming or what?"

Hearing footfalls behind her, Violet continued into the room. Opening the cabinet closest to the door, she pulled out a camping lantern, thankful that she'd remembered to replace the gas canisters the last time she'd been in town.

Violet had just lit the wick when she felt Tyson's hand on hers. "Not too bright... they're drawn to light."

Violet jerked her hand away, turning to face him. Her breath hitched in her throat at the sight of him in the soft light. He was almost exactly as she remembered him... well-proportioned, rugged, dark brown hair that had a will of its own—and those eyes...soft and hazel, like warm toffee left to muddle in the sun. He was the same, yet somehow, different.

"And who, exactly, are *they*?" she asked, forcing her gaze away as she opened another cabinet door, pulling out the whiskey. Grabbing two glasses from the shelf below, she plopped herself down at the kitchen table and filled the glasses. Tyson had always been partial to a bit of Tennessee Whiskey, at least from what she remembered.

Pushing a glass towards him, she watched as he turned around the chair across from her, straddling it, the light from the lantern playing over his features. *He is still a handsome devil,* she thought. *If you like the tall, dark, and unshaven type, that is,* she mentally added.

Apparently, based upon the tingling in her body, she still did.

Violet shifted uncomfortably in her chair. Taking a swig of the whiskey, she was grateful for the biting warmth it provided. If only it could erase the feelings that were now resurfacing, clouding her thoughts. Violet could see the pain written across Tyson's face as he drummed his fingers around the glass slowly.

Ever since she'd taken over the Jennings Hunting Lodge from her uncle a couple of years ago, she'd hardly set foot off the mountain. The lodge had a well-stocked larder, a lake out back for fishing, and plenty of game to hunt. This, along with the vegetable gardens at the side of the cabin, enabled her to be self-sufficient. Basically, she had everything she needed right here. Not to mention, it had made for a great hideaway after what had happened back home. It was somewhere she could be alone and heal in her own time, in her own way. As such, there was never any need to know what was going on in the world. It was perfect...until now.

Now, everything had changed. In a split second, with the arrival of this ghost from her past, one she'd thought she'd long since buried, he'd managed to turn her whole world upside down.

Clearing her throat, she waited for him to begin.

TYSON

Tyson studied her silently. She looked so beautiful, sitting there nursing her whiskey. It was enough to make a man forget his name, never mind anything else that would make a man care one iota about the rest of the world. Even now, after two long years, she still had the ability to tie his gut into knots. Tyson shook his head. *I need to focus,* he silently chastised himself.

"This is gonna sound crazy, but it's the truth—and for your sake, you need to listen, and listen carefully," he said calmly, as he took a swig of his whiskey. Quickly taking another sip to steady his nerves, he finally continued.

"The illness you heard about… it turned out to be worse than they thought. It affects almost everyone—something about it being caused by a comet colliding with the moon. At least, that's what the news reports said. The ones that were infected, died, and they died quickly, while others developed...special abilities."

In truth, yes, they died—but then, without warning, they re-animated. At first, it was like a bad zombie movie; yet it wasn't. It was worse. This was real life. They would come back all right, but what came back wasn't human. Not entirely. It was as if their brains had been re-wired, removing all traces of humanity. Their very souls had been eradicated. Their only purpose now was to hunt and kill their prey... the survivors. The lucky ones—they were stronger, more capable of defending themselves than others. Tyson and Drew happened to be two of the lucky ones. They had at least remained human.

"So, it's over?" she interjected. "They must have found a cure by now," she finished, silently awaiting an answer.

"Cure? No, there's no cure...other than a bullet to the brain for those undead things." He laughed dryly, watching as the color drained from her face. "Before the ones who died from the illness could even be buried, they came back to life," he tried to explain. Shaking his head, he continued. "Violet, what I've seen—" he stopped, unable to look at her. The image of his sister was forever etched into his memory.

Violet drained her glass and poured another in quick succession. "Go on," she croaked.

Tyson could see how hard it was for her to process all of the information he had given her in such a short period of time, but she had to know it all, for her sake. Cupping the glass in his hands, he stared at the amber liquid, as if it held all the answers to all of life's problems. *If only it were that simple.* Unfortunately, the simple life stopped being such a while ago. Now, life was simply a matter of survival.

Tyson sighed. "By the time people realized what was happening, it was too late. It had already spread out of control, and people were dropping like flies."

"Exactly what was happening?" Violet asked, gripping her glass.

"Things that should only exist in nightmares—they became a reality," he replied, tracing the rim of the glass with his forefinger. "It's like a bad science fiction horror movie out there. There were reports of the ghouls, or zombies, or whatever the hell they are. There were other things too, about the comet and the sickness, but communications failed before we found out any more information.

These *things* I've come up against; they attacked other people, mauled them. Hell, they ate them... took chunks of flesh outta them, which killed them. Then, just when we thought things couldn't get worse, those people turned into more creatures."

Tyson drained his drink and buried his head in his hands. The stark reality of what he'd had to face over the last few weeks was a far cry from his life before the comet. Before these creatures—or whatever they are, ever existed.

"So, how'd you end up here?" Violet asked softly, pouring him another drink.

Tyson lifted his head and looked at her. He felt his jaw twitch as a range of emotions played across his face.

"I was with my brother, our friends, Shawn, Nathan, Sully, and a few others—we were attacked just outside the city. So many people lost—dead." He placed his hands flat on the table as if to steady himself.

"Your brother, Drew, is he dead?" Violet asked softly, covering his hand with hers.

"No. Yes. Hell, I don't know." Tyson shook her hand off and jumped to his feet, moving to lean against the countertop. "We were separated a few days back, and I've been on my own since."

"What happened to Ellie?"

For a moment, Tyson said nothing. He simply stared at the shadows dancing, created by the light emanating from the lantern.

"She didn't make it, Violet. My sister got sick and she died. As soon as the shit hit the fan, we knew we had to leave. So, we started packing. Next thing we knew, Ellie was walking the halls, trying to take a chunk outta me. Drew had to…" Tyson hung his head and wrapped his arms around his body—as if to protect himself from darkness of his thoughts.

"Jesus, Ty, I'm sorry. I loved Ellie, you know that," Violet said tearfully. "You're not on your own anymore, Ty—not tonight, anyway. You can stay in one of the guest rooms. In the morning, we'll figure all of this out."

Standing, Violet began to walk past him when he suddenly grabbed her arm and pulled her to a stop. Losing her footing, she stumbled against his solid muscular frame. Instinctually, Tyson's hands flew to her waist to help steady her.

Looking into her eyes, he swore he saw a flicker of familiar emotions staring back. Though, before he could be sure, it was gone. Tyson tried to play it off as a trick of the light, but no matter how he tried to convince himself, it was enough—enough to send waves of desire coursing through his body.

As Violet's hands found their way to his chest, he took a deep, calming breath. *What I wouldn't give to wrap my hands up in her hair and pull her close, just to see if she still feels as good as she used to—minus the clothing, of course.* He bit his lip at the thought, allowing his imagination to wander.

M oving quickly to Kate's side, Drew awkwardly draped his arm across her shoulder. Gently stroking her thick, dark brown hair while holding her close, he could feel the grief wracking her ample body.

"How old was your daughter?" Drew asked softly.

"Ten. She had just turned ten a few days b–be—before it happened," she mumbled against his chest.

Drew knew that there was nothing he could say to make her feel better. Losing someone—anyone was hard, even at the best of times, but these days it was more horrific.

For himself, he would never be able to erase the memory of caving in his own sister's skull, no matter how hard he tried. It was a nightmare he would never awaken from. He wasn't sure if Tyson would ever forgive him for doing what he did. Hell, he didn't think he could ever forgive himself, but he hoped that one day he might be able to live with it. It was that hope which kept him going now. Hope for his brother's safety, and that of his group. Hope that this wasn't the end; that there was a life to be found beyond the pain, suffering, and death that they faced daily. There had to be hope, because without it, he may as well throw himself to those creatures and let them eat him alive.

The sudden sound of an unexplained crash just outside quickly drove them both toward the boarded-up window. In the fading light, they could faintly make out the shadows lurching across the road. Placing his finger to his lips, Drew slowly moved behind her. He only hoped the door would hold. There they stood, watching and waiting, not daring to move, let alone breathe.

As the main bulk of the pack staggered past the building the sounds of the dead reached a crescendo, some coming too close for comfort, stumbling against the wall. The noise slowly faded as the group thinned before finally dissipating. Just when they thought they were in the clear, a straggler paused briefly outside the window, growling, its decayed flesh flapping as it shuffled closer.

Placing his hand over Kate's mouth, Drew slowly pulled her away from the window. They couldn't risk that thing calling attention to their location. After several agonizing moments, the corpse retreated, dragging its feet as it tried to catch up with the others.

After removing his hand, Kate gratefully sucked in a huge breath of air. Looking into her eyes, Drew could see her relief reflected back. Taking a moment, they just stared at one another, both too reluctant to move. Instinctively lifting his hand, Drew gently brushed a strand of hair from her eyes, letting his knuckles graze her cheekbone before eventually coming to rest on her shoulder. A soft mewl of encouragement slipped from Kate's lips.

Gently pressing up against her until he had her sandwiched between him and the wall, Drew leaned further into her, their bodies lightly brushing together. Feeling her body tremble beneath him, her breathing became erratic. Staring into her eyes with such longing, it both frightened and excited him. Unable to control himself, his mouth descended, capturing hers with as much passion as he could muster.

Kate gasped, sliding her hands across his hips and pulling him flush against her body. Drew groaned. Deepening the kiss, he gently teased her tongue with his, nibbling at her lower lip. Capturing her hands, he held them firmly in place above her head with one hand, while the other slipped beneath her sweatshirt. He watched as both pleasure and pain flitted across her face as his fingers tweaked and caressed her already rock hard nipples.

Sliding his hand across her stomach he carefully eased it down the front of her jeans, pleased to find her already wet and more than ready for him. Eyes remaining locked, Drew pulled his hand free and slowly brought his fingers to his mouth. Grinding his erection against her, he watched as her eyes glazed over at the sight of him sucking her juices from his fingers, one by one. Leaning in, Drew kissed her, allowing her taste to coat her tongue.

KATE

Kate's head was spinning, her senses overwhelmed by this giant of a man that was currently ravishing her. She was desperate, and she needed him to put out the fire blazing through her body. There was no guarantee of what the dawn would bring, whether they would survive another day or not. All she knew for certain was that if tonight were to be her last, she was damn well going out with a bang.

For a moment, she forgot where she was—who she was, and the horrors that lie beyond the shadows. That's when the screams filled the air, shattering the illusion, and bringing her crashing back down to reality.

Drew was off her in a flash, quickly scanning the area outside through the boarded-up window. After adjusting her clothing, she silently moved to his side and tried to look for any signs of the source herself.

It was dark outside, too dark to really see what was happening, however, the screams painted enough of a picture for them. Slipping her hand into Drew's, she tried to offer some reassurance that they would be okay. He gently squeezed her hand once, before letting go and drawing his gun. Checking and double-checking it, he kept it at the ready.

For a moment, there was silence. However, the silence didn't last long before the howling began.

6 Shawn

S hawn hadn't gone far when he heard the gunfire from deep within the mall. Fear for his friend clouded his usually sound judgment as he ran blindly towards the source. Gun drawn and at the ready, he slid to a halt inside the bookstore, just in time to see Sully hit the ground.

"Sully!" Shawn roared, turning his attention to the shooter. Before the man could move toward him, Shawn tackled him to the ground. Taking advantage of the fact that his opponent was severely wounded, Shawn used every ounce of his strength to smash the guy's head against the tiled floor, repeatedly. It was the sound of a woman sobbing hysterically that finally brought him back to his senses.

Sickened by what he had done, Shawn quickly pushed himself to his feet. Turning on his heel, he was astonished to see a young blonde woman hunched over Sully, trying to stop the bleeding. Stepping over the fresh corpses, Shawn fell to his knees next to his friend.

"What the hell happened here?" Shawn hissed at the woman.

"He saved me...f–f—from them," she stuttered, pointing in the direction of the dead men strewn across the shop floor. "They were about to—" the words caught in her throat as the tears began to fall.

She didn't need to finish her sentence; Shawn knew full well what their intentions had been. The world had gone to hell, and the living were turning into animals.

"We've got to get Sully to the truck. You have to hold it together. I can't do this without you," Shawn said calmly. Throwing Sully over his shoulder, he grunted as he rose to his feet. *Damn, Sully needs to lay off the junk food he keeps scavenging.*

"Grab his gun and follow me," Shawn ordered. Making his way toward the store's entrance, Shawn prayed the woman was behind him. They needed to move quickly—and quietly.

Glancing back, he could see the woman grab the gun before quickly running after them. They made good time getting back to the main door and without further incident, which was a relief.

"Keep a look out while I get Sully in the truck, will ya?" Shawn barked, pointing toward a red pickup truck a few feet away. Lugging a still unconscious Sully to the vehicle, he placed him in the middle of the front seat and climbed in behind the wheel.

In the distance he could see a large group of undead freaks heading straight for them. Taking aim, Julie began picking them off, one by one. Still, they kept coming. Shawn wasn't sure what was more unnerving; the noise that they made and the sheer grotesqueness of them lurching and weaving towards them, or the knowledge of what would happen if they caught them.

"Get in!" Shawn yelled, leaning across Sully to open the passenger door.

Julie threw herself into the truck, simultaneously slamming the door and rolling up the window. Bracing himself, Shawn hit the gas and the truck took off, sending a couple of roamers flying.

It wasn't long before they were on the main road, heading towards the freeway. Breaking the silence, Julie asked, "Where are we going?"

He turned to find her attending to Sully by applying pressure on his wound.

"Back to our camp. We have a doctor there. Hopefully, he can help Sully."

They rode in silence most of the journey while occasionally chancing a look at his friend.

"I'm Julie, by the way. Julie Jackson," she offered, in an attempt to make conversation.

"Shawn Robertson," he replied gruffly, keeping his eyes on the road while deftly swerving around walking corpses.

"How long till we get to your camp?" she asked, pressing harder on Sully's wound.

"Not long; thirty minutes or so."

"We need to hurry, Shawn. He's losing a lot of blood," she hissed.

"Damn it! Just hang on, Sully. You hear me, you bastard. Hang on," Shawn yelled. White-knuckling the steering wheel, he floored the gas pedal.

Julie held onto Sully as the truck careened past abandoned vehicles and sideswiped a few undead creepers before hitting a stretch of open road.

Shawn knew time was running out. He had to get Sully back to their camp so that Fitzgerald could patch him up. Glancing at their companion, he couldn't help but wonder what her story was. She looked like she'd been through hell, but whether they could trust her, he just wasn't sure. Despite being beat up and filthy, he could tell that she was an attractive woman. In this day and age, it didn't mean squat if you couldn't handle yourself.

Thirty minutes later they pulled up to a warehouse on the outskirts of town. It was deserted, which is just the way they liked it. Jumping out of the truck, he ran to the side door, knocked four times at various intervals and ran back to help Julie pull Sully from the truck.

They had just gotten Sully out of the truck's cab, when the warehouse door opened and Nathan appeared. He didn't bombard Shawn with questions; he simply grabbed Sully's legs and helped Shawn carry him in. That was the great thing about Nathan; he was a man of action and few words.

"Fitzgerald, get your lazy ass over here. Sully's been shot," Shawn yelled, setting their friend down on his blanket.

"You finally get tired of his mouthing off to you?" Connor Fitzgerald joked, kneeling to examine the wound.

"Just patch him up, jackass," Shawn snapped, not in the mood to be jerked around.

"Sure thing, Detective," Connor said, throwing a mock salute in Shawn's direction.

Shawn stepped forward, wanting nothing more than to beat the cocky grin right off his face, but before he could reach him, Nathan grabbed his arm.

"He ain't worth it, Shawn."

Shawn forced himself to take a few deep, calming breaths. "Yeah. Come on, we've got some supplies in the truck. Help me unload them before it gets too dark?"

"Sure thing, buddy."

The two of them gathered the meager haul and stocked it in the corner of the room that sufficed as the kitchen. Grabbing the few medical supplies he'd scavenged, Shawn took them over to Connor.

"Who's the babe?" Connor asked, glancing up at Julie.

"None of your business. Get on with it," Shawn glared at the dark-haired man.

Connor ignored Shawn and flashed a smile at Julie before continuing to work on Sully. He had lost so much blood, Shawn wasn't sure they had gotten him back in time.

"The bullet went straight through so I've just stitched him up. We'll have to keep an eye on him for infection, but as long as he gets these antibiotics and rests up, he should be fine," Conner said, standing up.

"Thanks, Doc," Nathan said quietly. "We'll take turns watching him."

"Sure thing. Now, I best go see that our new friend doesn't have any injuries," Conner winked at them before heading over toward Julie.

Sitting down next to Sully, Shawn carefully covered him with a spare blanket. "You had to play the hero," he muttered more to Sully than to anyone else.

"That what happened?" Nathan asked, joining Shawn.

"Yeah. He found her—Julie...being attacked by some guys. So he went in, guns blazing, and took 'em out. All but the one who decided to clip his wing," Shawn explained.

"He's always been a good guy in that way. Hell, you know how he feels about people being nice to the womenfolk we come across. It's just the way he is."

"I know, Nathan, but one of these days it's gonna get him killed. Hell, it almost did today." Shawn sighed.

Nathan didn't say anything, he just stared at Sully's chest, watching him breath. *He has to know I'm right. Sully is going to get himself, or someone else, killed if he carried on with his Lone Ranger behavior,* Shawn thought to himself in exasperation.

A fearful cry from behind them had him on his feet instantly. Glancing over, he found Julie cowering from Connor, stark fear etched upon her face.

"Come on, honey, just let me have a look. It ain't nothing I haven't seen before," Connor laughed as he grabbed her shirt and tried to pull it off.

"Please, don't touch me. No!" Julie cried, struggling to get away.

Seeing red, Shawn strode over to them, placing himself in front of Julie, and knocked Connor on his ass with a single punch.

7

Tyson

Tyson had only meant to stop her so that he could thank her. He hadn't intended for her to end up in his arms, his hands clutching her shapely waist, her emerald eyes searching his for something—anything. However, when she touched him, placing her hands on his chest, it felt as though she were branding him. When she licked her lips, Tyson lost all sense of his surroundings. He forgot all about the hell he'd been through in the last few weeks. All he knew was that Violet was back in his arms, and he wanted desperately to lose himself in her softness. He wanted her. No...he needed her.

Leaning down, his lips hovered just a fraction above hers for a moment before their lips finally connected. Violet moaned softly, surrendering to his touch. The softness and warmth of her lips was intoxicating. Deepening the kiss, Tyson teased her lips apart with his tongue, pulling her body flush against his. Her hands moved up to encircle his neck, burying her fingers in his tousled hair. Instinctively, Tyson's hands slid down to cup her shapely behind, pulling her closer, allowing her to feel his arousal.

Realizing what was about to happen, he pulled away, his eyes sweeping her flushed face before he leaned in to whisper in her ear. "You'd best run off to bed, darlin', before we both do something we'd regret," Tyson growled huskily as he gently pushed her away.

Turning, Tyson placed his hands on the counter before taking a few deep breaths. He tried desperately to think of something, anything, to help diminish the erection straining painfully against his denim jeans. To be honest, he had expected her to run to safety, to get away as fast as she could. What he didn't expect was for her to slip her arms around his waist and hold onto him, as if her life depended upon it. This was dangerous territory—for both of them.

Violet hesitantly released her grasp as he turned to face her. What he found was her, staring at him, with that look on her face— the one that always drove him wild; the one that led them to do a hell of a lot more than just kiss.

Grabbing his shirt, she pulled him toward her, her hands sliding under the fabric and tracing his abs. He sucked in a deep breath as her fingers travelled lower, down his stomach, stopping just above his jeans. With nimble fingers, she carefully undid his belt buckle. Moments later, their clothes were strewn across the floor.

"Ty, I need you. Now," Violet purred, her lips working their way up his neck to nibble on his earlobe.

Tyson had never been able to resist her, and that fact had not changed, despite the years apart. He growled in acquiescence, scooping her up in his arms and carefully setting her down upon the kitchen table. Taking a couple of steps back, he took a moment to enjoy the view as the light from the lantern played over her body. Her curves were what he'd always loved about her. In the flickering light, he watched as her golden hair fell over her shoulders in waves, ending just above a generous pair of breasts. *She is just as beautiful as I remember.*

Reaching out, his fingers lightly teased her skin, running them up and down each side of the soft mounds of flesh. She moaned. Biting her lip as his fingers firmly squeezed a nipple, his mouth quickly descended upon the other. Not wasting any time, Tyson's hand slid lower, finally reaching the juncture of her thighs. Hungrily, his lips claimed hers. Making his way back up, his hands gently parted her legs before sliding his fingers deep into her wetness.

Moaning loudly, Violet arched her back as Tyson nibbled his way down her body, licking a trail of fire to his ultimate destination.

Grabbing her hips, Tyson arched her body upward, gently teasing her before finally diving in to her sweetness. Violet cried out as Tyson's mouth descended, his tongue swirling over her clit. Knowing her body like he did, even after all these years, his instincts told him that she was close to an orgasm. Not one to be denied, he dipped two fingers inside of her wetness, thrusting deeply, as he continued his oral assault upon her clit.

Violet tensed, her body balancing on the precipice just before wave after wave of pleasure sent her spiraling into ecstasy. Tyson relentlessly lapped up her juices as she came, trying to hold her still as her body shook from the intensity of her orgasm.

By the time her body had stopped shuddering, Violet could barely breathe. It was obvious that we had forgotten how good this could be—how good we could be.

Sitting up, Violet pulled Tyson towards her, desperate to taste herself on his lips. Kissing him, she ran her hands over his body before hooking her feet behind his legs, drawing him further into her. With one hand around his neck she used her other to slide down between them, encircling his arousal. Violet lightly, almost playfully, stroked him before carefully guiding him into her welcoming wetness. Wrapping her legs around his waist more tightly, she gave him even more access, taking him deeper inside herself.

Tyson gasped at the mere feeling. It had been so long. However, it wasn't long before instinct kicked in and he was picking her up and setting her down upon the chair so she could straddle him. He watched her through heavy, lust-filled eyes, fondling her breasts as she rode him slowly, sensually. With his hands on her hips, he guided her, helping to support her.

Violet must have known he couldn't last much longer as she began to move with more urgency, her nails digging into his shoulders, head thrown back. Sliding his hand down between their bodies, Tyson found her clit, rubbing it at a fevered pitch. The dueling sensations were enough to send Violet spiraling into another orgasm. The mere feeling of her wrapped around his shaft quickly triggered his own orgasm, as Violet collapsed against him. Her breath was ragged against his neck as she trembled from the force of their shared orgasms.

As reality came crashing back, neither of them wanted to move. Unfortunately, they both knew they couldn't stay like that forever. After all, there was no such thing as forever anymore. Before he could say anything, Violet eased herself away from him, gathered her clothes, and left the kitchen without a word.

That night, Drew couldn't sleep, so he kept watch at the window. The howling and screaming from earlier had him on edge. There was something in the air...it smelled different—stronger, more pungent. For some reason, his senses had been heightened lately...ever since he'd been forced to kill Ellie. Glancing over at Kate, there was just enough moonlight for him to see that she had her eyes closed. Whether she was sleeping or not, he wasn't certain.

Kate had withdrawn to the corner of the room once the howling had ceased. It was obvious to Drew that she was holding something back. There was more to this woman than just a pretty face and sexy curves. It had been a long time since he'd felt anything other than passing interest in a woman. His brother's failed marriage had taught him better than to get too involved with a woman. Especially one you barely knew. Less chance of getting your life turned upside down that way.

"You awake?" Drew asked softly, sitting down next to her.

"Yes. Just thinking," she replied, rubbing her temple.

"You got something you need to talk about, Kate?"

"You're a very astute man, Mr. Hawkins," she replied dryly.

"Nah, just good at reading people is all."

"There is something I should tell you. And you're probably not going to like it."

"Why don't you let me be the judge of that, sweetheart?"

Kate flushed at the mention of the pet name, which surprised him. She seemed to be a complicated mix of uncertainty and strength. Shaking his head, he settled against the wall and waited for her to talk.

"I was hired by the government for a special research and development project. Our team worked under the world's leading scientists in weaponized aerosols." She took a breath before continuing. "We were developing a virus that could be used against our enemies if we came under attack from foreign entities. But something went wrong; it fell into the wrong hands and was released into the water supply. The vapors somehow altered the atmosphere, as well as infecting humans. That is what caused all of this to happen. By the time we realized what was happening—it was too late."

"Wait—are you telling me that the government...that you...are the ones who started this whole thing?" Drew slowly got to his feet, anger and confusion waging a war within him as he tried to grasp everything she'd said.

"It was supposed to prevent something like this from happening. Not be the cause of it," Kate's voice cracked with emotion.

Drew was finding it hard to breathe. Remaining quiet, he stared blankly into the darkness.

"Drew?" Kate said softly.

"You killed my sister! She was sixteen—had her whole life ahead of her. Ellie died from the sickness and came back as one of those *things*. She attacked our brother...I had to—" Drew choked up, turning away from Kate. "I—I smashed her head in with a hammer."

"I'm sorry, Drew. We didn't know what would happen. We thought we were helping people, saving them from a future terrorist attack. We thought we were doing something good," she cried.

Drew spun around and glared at her. *How could one woman be so infuriating?* Clenching and unclenching his fists, he tried to calm down. The one thing he had never done was strike a woman, and he wasn't about to start now.

"Kate, how can you defend what you did? What your scientist friends did?" he spat.

"I can't defend it. I'm just trying to explain why we did what we did. We were following orders," she retorted, getting to her feet.

"Your little *experiment* killed people," Drew yelled, disgust and anger pulsing through every fibre of his being.

Drew, we had no idea that this would be the outcome." Kate sighed, "This was beyond anything we could have ever comprehended. It was a mistake; a terrible one. One I wish I'd never been a part of."

Drew snorted and turned his back on her.

"Don't you dare turn your back on me," Kate hissed, grabbing his arm. "What's done is done. I can't change that now, but I do know how to move forward…how to regain some semblance of a life…how to survive."

"What the hell are you talking about? There isn't any way out of this."

"Yes, there is. Once I realized what had happened, I began to notice certain things happening. People weren't just dying and coming back to life. There were some who developed certain abilities—abilities that could become the conduit to escape this hell we're now living in."

"Setting aside the fact that what you did, what you were a part of, was abhorrent—if you have a way out of this, spill it."

"These abilities are varied. I think they were created by the influx of radiation from the contents of the chemicals used, and only affect those with certain genetic traits. Those people are the ones with strength enough to survive this and forge some sort of future for the rest of the population."

"What abilities are you talking about?" he asked suspiciously. Considering he had experienced a few strange things happening to him lately, his interest was piqued.

"We didn't really have time to run many tests. We did notice a few people gained exceptional strength and some—changed."

KATE

A sudden flash of lightning drew Kate's attention to the window. Mere seconds after a thunderclap shook the dilapidated building, the rain came down. Hard. More lightning, followed closely by a series of thunderclaps, rocked Kate to her core. Thunderstorms had always both terrified her and left her in awe. *This is going to be a bad one. I can feel it,* she thought to herself. It was almost as if God were visibly showing his anger towards her in a wondrous and terrifying display of power.

Another flash of lightning illuminated the sky; only this time, she saw shadows moving within. *They're back.* The sounds of the undead might have been masked by the voracity of the storm, but they were out there. The horde must have circled back round. Lightning illuminated the sky once again and Kate's heart sank. There were dozens of those creatures out there.

"Kate, what changes exactly?" Tyson growled.

"Shh!" she hissed. Grabbing Tyson's arm and pulling him to the window, she whispered, "They're back."

"Damn it! We've gotta get out of here."

"How? There are too many of them and the storm's too bad."

"So, what, we just wait to get killed?" Drew snapped.

"And you'd rather do what? Offer us up on a silver platter in the middle of another fucking freak storm?" she spat.

There was no safe way out of this for them. Not right now anyway. Either way, they were probably dead. A knife, two guns between them, and a few rounds of ammo—it was possibly enough to take out a dozen, maybe more, if their aim was true. *We should have kept driving.*

"We're gonna have to just ride it out then." Drew sighed before beginning to move some of the furniture in front of the door. The wind was picking up and beginning to rattle the door, drawing more unwanted attention. Without another word, Kate set to work on securing the windows and checking the boards covering them.

"Thanks," he muttered, moving to stand beside her.

"No problem. It's my ass on the line here too, you know."

"Yeah. We need to finish what we were talking about, but now ain't the time."

"If we get out of this, I'll tell you anything you want to know," Kate said quietly.

"We will get out of this—that's a promise, sweetheart," Tyson replied.

Kate wasn't sure whom he was trying to convince, but she wasn't sure it was working.

Standing at the window, they both watched the storm rage on in all its glorious fury. Holding her hands to her ears as the thunder rattled the windows, she could tell the storm was getting worse. Unfortunately, that wasn't a deterrent for the undead. Every time lightning lit the sky, she saw more silhouettes than before. Before long, a swarm of the undead was surrounding them.

"What are we going to do?" she whispered, looking at Drew.

He shook his head and put his finger to his lips. Handing her a gun, it was his way of telling her that she should be prepared. Kate nodded, watching as he drew his revolver and positioned himself between her and the door. They had barricaded it as best they could, but it was an old building and it was taking a hell of a beating from Mother Nature right now.

Kate's breath hitched as the door rattled and shook. The noise from the mob of undead creatures now rivaled that of the storm. She was sure that they were done for when the door began to give. Drew motioned for her to have her gun at the ready and move to the back of the room. They stood, guns drawn, and backs to the wall, preparing for the worst when out of the blue, lightning struck a tree out front. It caught on fire before finally toppling over in slow motion, falling towards the building. Kate's heart sank as she watched through the window just before Drew pushed her down, shielding her body with his.

The tree took out the entire front of the building and just enough of those things, allowing them to make it to the motorbike. Kate pushed herself to her feet as Drew began to kick the debris out of their way. *He sure is strong; impossibly so,* Kate thought in observation.

"Kate, we have to go. Now!" Drew yelled above the noise of the storm and the falling debris.

She didn't waste any time arguing. Grabbing the backpack, she quickly followed him through the burning rubble. From the shadows, something jumped out at her and she put it down without hesitation. Firing off a few shots of his own, Drew continued to clear a path, quickly continuing toward the bike. Burning corpses followed in their wake, their scent alone speaking promises of dinner.

Moments later, they were carefully maneuvering his beat-up bike through the storm ravaged streets, searching for a safe haven to wait out the rest of the storm. Despite everything, at least they were still together.

Far better to be stuck with a guy who probably hates my guts, than be left to face those things on my own.

9

Shawn

Shawn stood over a prone Connor, fists clenched, ready to do more than just knock a few teeth loose. Hearing Julie cry only fuelled his rage. How many more times was Connor going to cross the line before they finally did something to stop him. Technically, the law no longer existed, but that didn't mean that everyone was free to do whatever they damn well pleased. The law was just something he couldn't forget.

He'd been a detective before the world changed and a damned good one at that. Shawn prided himself on his stellar career, commendations and meritorious promotions. Not only was he good at his job, but he was well liked too. Everyone could always count on him to help, no matter the time of day. It was just who he was. Now, faced with a potentially dangerous man who had a knack for talking himself out of the situations, Shawn wasn't sure what the outcome would be.

Leaning down, Shawn grabbed hold of Connor's shirt, hauling him to his feet in one fluid motion. "You go anywhere near this woman—hell, any woman under my protection ever again, and you will lose more than a tooth. You got it, jagoff?"

"Yeah, I got it," Connor replied snidely, spitting a glob of blood onto the floor. "Can you let go now, or do you have something else to say, *Detective*?"

"No, and if it were up to me, none of us would have to speak to you ever again."

"But it's not up to you, is it?" Connor smirked. "Your fearless leader isn't here to back you up."

"Believe me, the minute Drew gets back, we will be discussing you. That I can guarantee," Shawn snarled, roughly releasing Connor's shirt and shoving him away from them.

He waited, observing Connor as he scurried back to his makeshift tent. Before entering, the man grabbed hold of his daughter's arm and dragged her behind the material divider. Shawn felt sorry for the young girl, having such an asshole for a father. She deserved better, so much better.

"Thank you," Julie croaked, tearfully.

Shawn turned towards her. She was a trembling wreck. All he wanted to do was offer her some form of comfort, but considering all that she'd been through, he figured it was the last thing she'd want.

"You're welcome, Julie," he replied. "I'll show you where you can get cleaned up."

Wrapping her arms tightly around her body, she followed him to the wash area.

Shawn shook his head as he thought about the situation. He couldn't imagine what that woman must have been through—not only in the last few days, but since it had all began. She seemed broken, yet he could tell she was a fighter. If she weren't, she would have stayed in the bookshop and waited for death to come to her. The fact that she had come with them showed an inner strength that few people had these days. That was something he greatly admired.

Heading toward a cordoned off area on the far side of the warehouse, Shawn pointed to the corner. "There's a few towels, some soap, and a bucket of water for rinsing," Shawn said softly. "I'll see about finding you some clean clothes."

"Thank you," Julie replied, gratefully picking up a towel and dipping it in the cool water. Placing the wet cloth to her face, she wiped furiously, leaving Shawn to wonder if she was attempting to remove more than just the dirt and blood that caked her pale skin. Quietly, he backed away and headed towards the storage area.

Rummaging through the boxes of clothes, he searched for something suitable for Julie. It didn't take long for him to find some jeans and a t-shirt that looked about the right size. They had lucked out a few weeks ago while scavenging and had scored bags of clothes and canned foods. *If only the food lasted as long as the clothes*, Shawn thought to himself as he made his way back.

"Hey baby, what ya doing?" a female voice purred behind him.

Shawn grimaced. The last thing he needed to deal with right now was Kai. The bitch latched on to whomever she figured would best serve her needs. Lately, he was the one she had set her sights on.

"Come on, baby, talk to me," she persisted, snaking a hand around to cup his cock through his jeans.

He pushed her away without hesitation. "Dammit, woman! Get it through your thick head—I don't want anything to do with you."

"You're nothing but a bastard, Shawn. You know that." Kai shrieked, slapping him hard across the face.

"At least I'm an honest one. You're only good for one thing, Kai…and you're running out of options. If I were you, I'd be real careful about how you treat the people you need in order to survive."

"You'll come crawling back to me as soon as the new bitch refuses you. Just you wait."

"Darlin, I wouldn't go near you with a ten-foot pole…even if my life depended upon it," he replied, calmly grabbing the clothes, and walking away from the fuming woman.

Shawn flashed a smile across the room to Nathan who just shook his head at the drama. Nathan had been lucky enough to avoid Kai's grasp, while others had quickly fallen for her obvious charms.

Making his way toward the wash area, he came to a sudden stop as he approached. Julie was standing with her back towards him, her shirt off, straining to wash her back—a back which was covered in welts and bruises. Her arms were in a similar condition. The woman had obviously been used as a punching bag. Not wanting to startle her, he stepped back behind the sheet and cleared his throat.

"Julie, I found some clothes for you. I'm just going to slip them under the sheet, okay?"

"Thank you, Shawn. I'll be out in a minute," she replied.

Pushing the clothes under the sheet, he sauntered over toward Nathan, anger burning a hole in his gut. "I'm glad I smashed that guy's head in now."

Nathan looked up. "What are you talking about?"

"She's covered in bruises and welts. They beat the crap outta her, Nate."

"Damn," Nathan hissed. "I would have done a lot worse than that had I been the one to find em."

"You realize we're gonna have to keep an eye on her? Fitzgerald seems a little too interested in her for my liking," Shawn said quietly.

"After what happened to Hannah a few weeks ago, I think we need to do more than that."

"We don't know what *really* happened to her. We all think we know, but none of us will ever know the whole story."

"For fuck's sake, Shawn—she killed herself because he raped her," Nathan said angrily.

"Nathan, we don't know that for sure. And until we do, we watch him closely, and we wait. You got it?"

"Yeah, I got it. I'm going out on rounds. You watch her first, okay?" Nathan grabbed his rifle before heading out the door.

Turning his attention to Sully, Shawn sighed, prodding him gently with his boot. "You'd better wake up soon, bro. I'm gonna need some backup if the shit hits the fan."

"Shawn?" Julie appeared at his side, kneeling next to Sully.

"Hey, how are you feeling?" Shawn asked, handing her a bottle of water.

"A bit sore, but cleaner than I've been in quite a while. Thank you for the clothes. I'll pay you back...somehow," she promised, averting her eyes.

"Don't worry about it. You don't owe us a thing. You got it?" he replied firmly. He didn't like the thought of her feeling as though they'd take advantage of her for the price of a shirt.

She smiled tentatively in acknowledgment. "Is Sully going to be okay?" she asked, her voice laced with concern.

"Luckily, the bullet was a through and through. Fitzgerald said he'd be fine. He better pray Sully pulls through, or he'll have me to deal with."

"I don't like him—your doctor. There's something...off about him."

"Yeah, I know. But he's handy to have around, especially with this fool getting himself into all sorts of scrapes time and time again."

"I owe Sully my life, Shawn. I just hope he wakes up so I can thank him properly," she said, stroking Sully's hair away from his face.

Suddenly, Nathan came barreling in through the door, "There's a storm coming—and fast."

"How soon?" Shawn asked, jumping to his feet.

Before Nathan could answer, a large thunderclap shook the air. Shawn felt dread wash over him. They had barely survived the last storm, the storm that had taken Hannah. He wasn't going to lose anyone else. Not if he could help it.

10
Tyson

Tyson could sense that Violet had returned to the room. He could feel her eyes on him. Prolonging the inevitable conversation that could no longer be avoided, he took his time getting dressed.

"It wasn't your fault, you know," he said softly, without turning around. "It wasn't mine either. It just happened."

"I know," she replied, choking up. "It was just easier to blame one another than it was to accept the loss of our baby girl."

He didn't—he couldn't look at her. He simply stared at the wall, remembering each detail, as if it had just happened.

"She would have been three-years-old, our little Grace."

Tyson's heart ached. That day had changed their lives. Their one-year-old daughter had been killed in a car crash, one that they had somehow managed to walk away from, relatively unscathed. Arguments followed, then silence, and eventually avoidance. After a while, Violet couldn't handle it anymore. She packed up and left, without so much as a goodbye. In the blink of an eye, Tyson lost the two most important girls in his life.

Tyson tried desperately to choke back the emotions that threatened to break down the walls around his heart. Sometimes it was best to leave the past buried where it belonged—in the past.

Now is not the time to go down that road, he thought to himself. Tyson looked at Violet, unsure of everything—except for one thing––*he loved her*. He'd never stopped loving her.

Looking at Violet, her silence spoke volumes. He went to her, pulling her into his arms and holding her as she cried. Stroking her hair, he held her until her tears ran dry.

He tilted her face up towards his, capturing her lips tenderly. Tyson kissed her as though it were his last chance to savour her sweetness.

Without warning, a thump startled them, forcing them apart. Pushing her behind him, he faced the kitchen door.

"Be quiet," he hissed, turning off the lantern.

Creeping toward the window, he hitched back the curtain a sliver. His stomach lurched when he saw what lay beyond.

The yard was crawling with the undead. Dozens of drooling, bloodied freaks were heading straight for the cabin. He didn't wait to look for any other dangers—not that he knew what to look for. Right now, they were all he knew.

They had to make a run for it.

Quickly, but silently, he made his way to Violet, grabbed her arm, and dragged her through the cabin, toward the front door. He paused, checking the front porch. It was clear—for now.

"We have to go—now," he whispered, yanking her jacket from behind the door and thrusting it in her arms.

"But—the cabin! I—I can't just leave..." Violet stammered as Tyson practically forced her into her jacket.

"You don't get it, do you? Your backyard is filled with everything I just told you about, looking to have us for dinner." Tyson dragged her to the kitchen window. Pulling the curtain aside, he shoved her up against the window, letting her see for herself the danger they were in.

She gasped, flinching at the sight before her. "Oh my God!" Violet stepped back and looked up at Tyson. He could see the fear and confusion in her eyes.

"Okay, just let me grab some things," she whispered.

"There's no time," he snapped. "If we don't go now, we might as well serve ourselves up on a plate and let them at us." Tyson hurried back to the front door to retrieve his backpack with Violet on his heels.

Grabbing a few things on the way, she began stuffing them into her pockets. Detouring momentarily, she ducked into the hall closet before joining Tyson at the front door.

"I'm not going anywhere without these," she said, holding up two shotguns in gun slipcases.

Handing one to Tyson, he asked, "Any ammo?"

"A few boxes," Violet replied, handing him the bag of ammunition.

Tyson stuffed the bag in his backpack before helping her put it on. "You'll have to wear it if you're going to ride pillion, sweetheart." With one final check, he made sure the straps were fastened securely.

"We're going to make a run for it. Here, take this." Tyson handed her his revolver. "Once I get the bike fired up, you hop on, and then we're outta here. Till then, you fire at anything that comes our way."

VIOLET

Violet slipped the gun case over her shoulder and checked the revolver, making sure the safety was off.

They were just exiting the cabin when they heard glass breaking at the other end of the cabin. The damn things had gotten in. They had just made it down the porch steps when Violet saw them. Those things were materializing from all corners. Aiming the gun, she fired one shot after the other. Her shots were good. The corpses crumpled to the ground in a bloody heap, one on top of the other. She was so intent on getting the kill shots, Violet didn't notice more of them coming up behind her until they grabbed at her. She cried out, twisting, and turning, trying to free herself from their grasp.

She saw Tyson abandon the motorbike and raise his shotgun, taking a couple of them out.

Violet was struggling with the corpses and losing. She couldn't get a clean shot. Violet watched as Tyson pulled his knife from his belt and whacked one of the creatures with the butt of his shotgun, knocking it away from Violet, before slamming his knife into its skull. The blade made a wet, slurping noise as he retracted it. The thing crumpled to the ground, the look on its face one of almost comical surprise as its body contorted at his feet. Now able to move, Violet managed to shoot the remaining corpse as it launched itself at her. She dropped, rolling out of its reach as it fell. Pulling Violet to her feet, Tyson turned towards the bike, only to find more of the creatures staggering towards them.

"The pickup truck! Quick!" Violet yelled, running for the side of the cabin.

"Keys?" he yelled back, jogging after her.

"In the truck," Violet said breathlessly. Stopping next to the pickup, she removed the backpack and gun slip before wrenching the door open. Meanwhile, Tyson was firing rounds at a few corpses that were too close for comfort.

"Get in!" Violet yelled, tossing the gear into the truck before climbing in.

Tyson rapidly followed suit. Seconds later, they were barreling down the mountainside away from the swarm of corpses that had descended upon the cabin.

"Vi, slow down," Tyson said calmly.

She was easily doing eighty and he was holding onto the dash as they hit another bump in the road, momentarily launching them into the air.

Mentally giving him the middle finger, Violet eased off the accelerator and put her foot on the brake.

"Did you want to drive?" she snapped.

"No...just go easy, will you?" Tyson said, his voice wrought with frustration.

They travelled in silence for a while until they hit a crossroads. Stopping the truck, she turned toward him. She was calm now—as calm as she could be, considering the events of the last few hours.

"Which way?" she asked.

He stared back at her in silence. She could only imagine what was playing through his mind.

"Turn right. If I know my brother, he would have headed in that direction. If we can find him, we may stand a chance of surviving."

"Okay. Right it is," Violet nodded, reaching out to squeeze Tyson's hand. Heaven help her, but right now all they had was one another. They were stuck with each other, for better or worse.

She chuckled softly to herself. *We may as well be married again.*

The last few hours had been a rollercoaster of emotions and circumstances that had left her head spinning. Neither knew what lay ahead of them. Glancing over at Tyson and seeing him smile sadly at her, gave her a sense of peace, knowing that at least they were together. Somehow, they had been given a second chance...and alive and together was better than dead and alone. Violet smiled at her ex-husband before turning her attention back to the road and the long journey that lie ahead of them. All the while, she tried desperately to ignore the burning sensation spreading through her lower back.

11

Drew

Kate held onto him tightly as the bike slid around the corner. They were free of the swarm, but the rain was still lashing down. Thunder and lightning seemed to follow them as they sped away from the burning building. His pulse raced as lightning struck a tree near them. *We can't stay out here much longer*, Drew thought, his attention focused on maneuvering the bike through debris and dead bodies.

The storm continued to worsen as they drove, the headlight providing minimal light in the obsidian night, making their journey tedious and nerve-wracking. Drew was tired and worried. Not only was he out in the open, in the middle of another freak storm, he was also riding with a woman he wasn't sure he could trust. A woman that made him feel things he hadn't felt in years. He wasn't sure what concerned him the most—her involvement in the death of God knew how many people, or that he wanted to rip her clothes off and fuck her till they were both spent and delirious.

If the situation weren't so grave, he probably would have laughed at his foolishness. However, he knew better than to fall for a woman as smart and beautiful as the one clinging to him. No matter how good her body felt pressed against his, with her arms wrapped tightly around his waist. His cock throbbed in acknowledgement of the lust weaving its way through his body. He couldn't deny his physical attraction to her, but still…he was wary. There was more to her than she was letting on, and there was nothing he detested more than secrets and being lied to.

As they turned a corner, the beam from the headlight was enough to reassure Drew—they were nearing his camp. *Another few miles and we'll be home free.* Just then, lightning struck the tree line ahead of them, sending wooden missiles flying past them when a tree exploded. Kate's grip on his waist tightened in response as he dodged and swerved around the debris.

Just when he thought they were clear, another swarm appeared from the side of the road and moved towards them. Drew sped up to outrun them, but there were too many of them. The road was completely blocked. With no other choice but to take the long way around, he quickly spun the bike around and sped back in the direction they had come from.

Drew could feel the terror radiating off of Kate as her clutch on him tightened. If the situation were any different, he would have pulled over and reassured her. Unfortunately, now was not the time for tenderness, no matter how much he wanted to wrap her in his arms. One way or another, they would get out of this.

Taking one of the corners so suddenly, Drew didn't even notice the tree falling, until it was almost upon them. He swerved, sending the bike skidding while they were hurtled off into the grass embankment. For a split second, he was sure that this was it—this is how he was going to die.

Exhausted, Drew laid on wet grass for longer than he would have normally felt comfortable. All of this running—searching for Tyson, for food and shelter—it was his life now. A life he had never been prepared for, but one that suited him, according to Shawn. Pushing himself to his feet, he paused to get his bearings. Across the road from him lay the abandoned bike, its tires still spinning. Only feet away, stood Kate. But she wasn't alone.

Drawing his gun, he set off running towards Kate, gritting his teeth as pain reverberated through his skull. He wasn't about to lose her, regardless of his feelings, or despite them. He wouldn't lose another person. Lifting his arm, he swung at the shadow holding onto Kate. The force sent the figure flying with a grunt. Drew turned in time to watch Kate swing around, her leg sweeping the other shadow off its feet. He grabbed her arm and they started towards the bike.

"Wait," a woman's voice called out. "We just want to help."

Kate stopped and turned back in time to see the shadows getting to their feet. A flash of light from above revealed a man and a woman, hands held up, moving toward them.

"That's far enough," Drew shouted, aiming the gun in their direction.

"I'm Megan. This is my brother, Max," the woman yelled. "We have a vehicle and gas."

Drew glanced at Kate and then at the bike. Anyone with eyes could tell the bike was trashed. They wouldn't be going anywhere on it. Placing her hand on his arm, Kate squeezed, reassuring him. They didn't have any choice but to go with the siblings if they intended to survive past sun-up.

"Drew, we should go with them. We don't have a choice," Kate said, trying to reason with him.

"How do you know we can trust them?" he replied. He didn't trust people easily. Being with one person he didn't fully trust was one thing, adding two more—that was a recipe for disaster.

"I don't, but they don't know they can trust us either. Yet, here they are, offering us a ride."

Drew wasn't sold on the idea, but time was running out.

"Look, you can come with us or you can stay here. Either way is cool with us," Max shouted. "What ever you choose, it's got to be now."

Not wasting time, Max grabbed his sister and began to walk away, not looking back to see if they were following.

The storm reached a crescendo that sent Kate scuttling closer towards Drew. Tugging on Drew's arm, she silently urged him to make a decision.

He sighed, knowing that going with the mysterious siblings was the only option they had right now. Starting after them, Drew pulled Kate along as they ran to catch up. Lightning filtered through the sky, lighting up their surroundings, and alerting them to the approaching group of creatures. Drew and Kate had just caught up when Max started the engine of his Jeep. Flinging open the back door, he shoved Kate in before throwing himself in after her. Quickly pulling the door shut, the vehicle sped away.

"Glad you decided to join us," Max drawled, peering into the rear view mirror at them briefly before focusing on dodging a group of undead creatures.

"Thanks for the lift," Drew replied sullenly. Putting his life into the hands of others was something he felt distinctly uncomfortable with. He was a leader, someone others turned to, not the one who got rescued.

"So, where were you headed?" Megan asked, turning slightly in the front seat to look at them, a smile on her face.

"Back to my camp," Drew replied. "If you could drop us near there, we'd appreciate it."

"Do you have somewhere to go?" Kate asked the siblings; blatantly ignoring the daggers Drew was mentally sending her.

"No, we lost our group a few days back to a swarm. We were lucky to get out." Megan said, tying her hair back.

"We were going to head for the coast," Max added.

Kate nudged Drew and he ever so slightly shook his head. Not to be ignored, Kate nudged him again. He knew he'd regret this, but they needed numbers and Max had a plan, which was something they hadn't had in a long time.

"Why don't you join our group—we could both use the extra numbers if the coast is the destination," Drew finally suggested.

Before Max could answer, the dead appeared in front of them, blocking the road ahead.

12
Shawn

S hawn watched as Nathan glanced back, making sure he was still
following him to the door. After securing the front of the
building, as best they could, they quickly returned to Julie and Sully.

"This old building isn't going to last through many more of
these storms." Shawn sighed, crouching down next to Sully.

"We're gonna have to move to safer ground, eventually. May as
well be sooner rather than later," Nathan suggested, moving to stand
next to Julie.

"Yeah, but we need numbers in order to move safely. And you know damn well that Drew isn't gonna move too far until he finds his brother," Shawn replied, running a hand over his head.

"Well, we best pray that Tyson shows up, and soon, or else we'll all be dead," Nathan said gravely.

Shawn hoped that Drew had found his brother and that they would return, so they could start making plans and doing something––something other than hiding. That was what frustrated him the most. He was a man of action; he needed a plan, a destination. Staying in one place, holed up, and hoping for the best was not his way of taking care of things. They had given Drew the benefit of the doubt, and more than enough time to find Tyson. Now it was time for Drew to realize that he couldn't risk all of their lives, in hope of finding his brother.

"Damn, what bus hit me?" Sully suddenly groaned.

All eyes turned to him as he struggled to sit up.

"Don't push yourself, you've been shot," Julie said softly. Kneeling beside him, she gently pushed him back down. "You need to rest."

"Best do what the lady says, bro," Nathan laughed. "Bout damn time you listened to someone."

"Glad you're still with us, Sully," Shawn said gruffly, patting him on the leg. "It's not the same without you buzzing around, annoying everyone."

"Yeah, I knew you'd miss me if anything happened to me," Sully joked weakly, coughing from the effort.

"Sure, keep on believing that, bro." Shawn shared a slight smile with Nathan.

He was glad that his friend felt well enough to joke around. They'd had a narrow escape, but next time they might not be so lucky.

Once he was lying back down, Julie hurried to the bathing area, returning with a damp cloth. Kneeling beside Sully, she carefully washed the dirt and blood from his face, blatantly avoiding eye contact.

"It's Julie, right?" Sully rasped.

"Y—yes," she stammered, almost dropping the cloth when he placed a hand over hers.

"Glad you're okay, Julie," he said, closing his eyes.

Nathan exchanged a knowing look with Shawn. The poor woman was smitten with their Sully. *Hell, it may do him some good to have a decent woman around to show him some love and affection. Right now, though, we have more important things to worry about than Sully's love life.*

"Nathan, we should gather the others towards the rear of the building; it's the safest place to wait out the storm."

Nathan nodded. "You're probably right. Let's get Sully moved first, then we'll get the others settled."

They spent a better part of the next hour moving supplies and people to the back of the warehouse to wait out the storm. There weren't that many of them left, since the incident on the road that had separated most of them. There were only nine of them now, including Julie. The others had either died or had disappeared.

"Where are Fitzgerald and his girl?" Nathan asked, looking around and not seeing the odd pair.

Maddie was as fair as Connor was dark. Side by side they certainly didn't resemble father and daughter, which had always been a red light to Shawn but he wasn't one to stick his nose in other people's affairs.

"I haven't seen them since earlier."

"You want me to get them?" Nathan asked.

"Nah, I'll go," Shawn replied, heading for Fitzgerald's makeshift tent.

As Shawn approached the makeshift tent, the sounds of crying could clearly be heard. Ripping open the sheet covering the entrance, Shawn was shocked to find Connor on top of Maddie. It took him less than a second to process what he was seeing before grabbing hold of Connor and dragging him away from her. He threw the man against the wall, his fist repeatedly connecting with Connor's face. Every punch he landed was for Maddie, and for Hannah, and any other girl he had placed his vile hands on.

"Shawn, what the hell?" Nathan pushed him away from the bloody mess of a man, putting himself between them.

"I'm going to kill him," Shawn snarled. "Get out of my way, Nathan."

"No. What the hell is going on?" Nathan asked, standing firm.

"The bastard was raping his daughter," Shawn spat, the words tasting like bile on his tongue.

He glanced over at Maddie. She was sitting in the corner with her arms wrapped tightly around herself. She was disheveled, sobbing, and scared.

"Julie, can you come here?" Shawn called across the room.

"What's wrong?" Julie asked. Stopping short, she glanced fearfully at the scene before her.

"Please take Maddie and go wait with Sully. We need to have a little more of a *talk* with Fitzgerald here," Shawn said, his voice cold and hard.

Shawn looked at Nathan. His friend's face was fury personified. Nathan nodded and stepped back.

He waited until Julie and the girl were gone before turning toward the bloody man crumpled up on the floor. Without warning, he gave Connor a good hard kick, his boot connecting with the man's groin area. Connor cried out, grabbing his exposed crotch, and rolling over in agony.

"You bastard. You worthless, low-life piece of shit, scum," Shawn yelled. "Your own daughter? How could you?" he shouted, rearing back for another kick.

"Wait," Connor cried. "She's not my real daughter...she's my stepdaughter."

"And what? You think that makes it any more acceptable, asshole? She's thirteen-years-old! For fuck's sake, she's a child. She trusted you and you fucking abused her." Shawn leaned down and grabbed him by the collar of his shirt. "You did the same thing to

Hannah, didn't you? She was fifteen, jackass. She was alone and you took advantage of her. I should have killed you the minute I suspected something was wrong with you."

"You wouldn't. You don't have the balls to kill me," Connor dared.

"You'd be surprised what I'm capable of doing, Fitzgerald," Shawn replied. Pulling his gun from its holster and holding it against Connor's temple, he smiled as he cocked the gun.

13

Tyson

Tyson groaned as his head smacked against the window of the truck, waking him with a start. Rubbing his head, he attempted to stretch his large frame as best he could in the confines of the cab. It was still dark—only now, it was raining too.

"How long was I asleep?" he asked groggily.

"Not too long, about an hour or so," Violet replied. "There's a storm up ahead."

"Damn," Tyson muttered, sitting up straight.

Violet was driving slowly, carefully avoiding abandoned vehicles, as well as the dead. They still had several hours to go before sun-up. *Hopefully we have enough gas to get to Drew.*

Feeling the call of nature, Tyson uncomfortably shifted in his seat. *We have to pull over eventually; may as well be sooner, rather than later*, he thought to himself.

"Vi, pull up just ahead, would you?" Tyson asked.

"What's up?" Violet shot a quick glance at Tyson, confusion evident on her face.

"I have to take a leak," he said, flashing her a smile.

"Pig." Violet chuckled, shaking her head. Slowing down, she pulled the truck over to the side of the road and left the engine running as she threw it into park.

"You still love me regardless," he said cockily. Hopping out, he quickly made his way toward the rear of the truck to take care of business.

The sound of a woman's screams suddenly filled the air just as he was zipping up. Quickly drawing his gun, he spun around, unable to see anything.

"Ty?" Violet called out.

"Stay in the truck, Violet," Tyson said sharply as he strode back around to the passenger door. Leaning in, he blindly reached for his backpack and began digging around inside before finally finding his flashlight.

"What's going on?" Violet asked, her voice shaky.

"I don't know, stay here."

"Ty, we should get out of here." The unease was evident in her voice.

"Violet, if there's someone out there that needs help, I'm not going to just walk away. Now, stay here," Tyson said firmly before turning the flashlight on and quietly shutting the door.

He knew she'd be mad at him for leaving her alone, but he couldn't just ignore someone's pleas for help. Hearing the scream again, he strode towards the sound, away from the truck and into the darkness.

Not knowing what to expect, Tyson ran towards the sound, his revolver at the ready. Darting glances at the abandoned vehicles, he hurriedly moved past them. It wasn't long before he realized the screams were coming from within the woods. Entering the tree line with trepidation, he silently prayed for more light. As if the heavens had heard him, the lightning answered his prayer. Ahead of him, the flash of light allowed him to make out a group of people surrounding three others slightly ahead of him. Sneaking closer, he took his time, careful to remain hidden. There were five men standing in a circle, surrounding two women and an older man. From what Tyson could make out in the low light, the older man appeared to be unconscious.

Tyson could hazard a guess as to what these men were planning for the women. It was the way of the world now. However, it wasn't his way and it never would be. One thing his mama had taught him was to respect women, to protect them, and care for them. Tightening his grip on his gun, he took aim, carefully planning his attack. He wouldn't have a lot of time, so he had to be quick and accurate. He couldn't afford to waste ammo.

One of the men lunged for the woman nearest to him. Lightning flashed and Tyson made his move. He quickly managed to pick three of them off before the other two even realized what was happening. Unable to see clearly, one of them launched himself in Tyson's direction, providing an easy target. Tyson easily eliminated the guy before he got close. The remaining man, knowing the odds were against him, quickly moved to use one of the woman as a shield. Fortunately, she was too quick for him. Sweeping his legs out from under him, she picked up a nearby rock and brought it down upon the man's head repeatedly, until it was nothing more than a bloody mess.

"Kelly—he's dead," the other woman whispered, gently placing a hand on her shoulder. The woman dropped the rock and crawled towards the unconscious man.

"Dad?" she cried, shaking the prone man.

The other woman turned to face Tyson. "Thank you. We thought we were dead."

"We need to get outta here," he said, indicating some approaching corpses.

Glancing in the direction he had indicated, the woman hurriedly moved to help Kelly haul her dad to his feet while Tyson fired at the living dead. Taking aim, he pulled the trigger. *Nothing.* He was out of ammo. The final corpse bobbed and weaved as it charged forward on unsteady feet. Holstering his gun, Tyson removed the hunting knife from his belt and launched himself at the creature. Knocking the thing to the ground, he drove the knife deeply into its brain. Yanking the blade free, Tyson pushed himself to his feet and sheathed his knife. Turning, he found the two women staring at him, uncertain of what to do, while Kelly's father was propped between them.

Tyson sighed. *The last thing we need is more people to watch, but I can't just leave them here. Not with the storm worsening.*

"You can either come with me or you can stay here and die?" Tyson offered bluntly, walking toward them. He didn't wait for them to answer. Grabbing hold of the older, stockier man, and heaving him over his shoulder, he grit his teeth and made his way back toward the road with the women on his heels.

VIOLET

Violet was afraid, not only for Tyson, but for herself also. Reaching back, she gently lifted her shirt. The burning sensation was spreading. Cautiously pressing her hand against her skin, she instantly pulled it away. Her skin was so hot to the touch that it appeared to burn her hand. Pulling her shirt down, she leaned back against the cool leather. It only took a few moments for her to realize her hand was sticky.

Reaching into the glove box, she pulled out the spare flashlight before taking a deep breath and flicking it on. Her heart sank as she stared at the blood covering her hand. She frantically wiped her hand on her jeans and shoved the flashlight back in the glove box before shutting it. Violet knew she couldn't ignore it forever, but she hoped she could put off telling Tyson until they found his brother.

Opening the door, she slipped out of the truck, hoping to see Tyson. The storm was getting worse and they weren't safe just sitting there. Rain lashed down, providing welcome relief against the stinging sensation in her back. Meanwhile, thunder rolled across the sky, followed seconds later by a severe flash of lightning. She started, ducking back into the truck and shutting the door. *At least I'm safe in the vehicle—for now anyway.*

Violet continued to sit in silence and the storm raged on around her. She was on edge. Tyson had been gone far too long. The lightning flashes were more frequent, the thunderclaps deafening, and the rain torrential. Visibility was near non-existent, despite turning the wipers on full. As much as she wanted to, Violet didn't dare turn on the headlights for fear of attracting the undead creatures she was certain were roaming the road.

Damn. Where the hell is Tyson? Violet turned to look out the rear window, wincing as the burning flesh on her back pulled with the action. A noise suddenly drew her attention back to the front of the vehicle. She briefly considered leaving the truck, but the darkness, combined with the storm convinced her otherwise. Unable to see anything through the darkness, she damn near jumped out of her skin when the back doors flung open and strange people clambered in. Before she could react, Tyson jumped into the passenger seat.

"We need to go. Now," Tyson shouted, slamming his door shut.

"What the hell is going on, Ty? Who are these people?" Violet asked, her voice more high-pitched than normal.

"Just drive! I'll fill you in later," he snapped.

"Yes, sir," Violet muttered, before throwing the truck into gear. Making her way back onto the road, they began winding around the abandoned vehicles and dead creepers until they hit a stretch of road that was clear. Still she drove slowly, not willing to risk skidding out on the rain slick roads.

"How's he doing?" Tyson asked as he turned to face their passengers. Taking a moment to take in their features, he could see that the man resembled a greyer Sylvester Stallone, especially in build, with similar facial features, while his daughter was a smaller, slimmer redhead. The other woman had a rich, dark complexion with very short black hair and a don't-fuck-with-me expression upon her face.

"He's coming around," the African American woman replied.

"Good. Y'all got names?" Tyson asked.

"I'm Sam—Samantha Harris," the woman replied. "This is my girlfriend, Kelly, and her father, Duke Brandon."

"Nice to meet, y'all, though I wish it were under better circumstances," Tyson replied dryly. "I'm Tyson Hawkins and this is my wife, Violet."

"Ex-wife," Violet reminded him.

Violet could feel his eyes on her. Despite her lapse in judgment earlier, and her still very much existent love for him, she couldn't let him forget that they weren't back together just because they had slept together.

"I don't think that matters now, Vi—considering," Tyson said softly, placing his hand lightly on her arm.

She glanced at him briefly, her heart pounding.

"Look out!" Sam screamed.

Violet turned her attention back to the road, just in time to see a tree crashing onto the road ahead of them. She did the only thing she could…she hit the brakes.

14

Drew

"Hold on," Max yelled, swerving to avoid the creatures as best he could. There were too many of them to safely get through.

"Time for plan B?" Megan asked as she reached beneath the passenger seat.

"Hit it, sis!" Max yelled before hitting the brakes and spinning the vehicle around.

Pulling out a semi-automatic machine gun, Megan swung open her door and started firing into the crowd of freaks. The gunfire drew enough of them to one side of the road, allowing Max to drive through. Hitting the gas, the truck shot through what was left of the undead.

"Hot damn!" Megan yelled, slamming her door shut and placing the spent weapon beneath her seat.

"Nice going, sis," Max said, his concentration fully focused on the road ahead and avoiding getting jammed up by dead bodies.

"Piece of cake," Megan replied, laughing.

The road behind them was as clear as it could be and the road ahead even clearer.

"So, where's this camp of yours, Drew?" Max asked.

Drew was still uncertain of his decision to join forces with them, and no one could blame him. These days, you had to be just as afraid of the living as you were the dead...and anything else that was out there. But, eventually, they may need one another.

"We're holed up in an old warehouse about thirty minutes away. It was the best we could do with the numbers we had at the time," Drew replied, knowing that by the time he returned, their numbers very well could be even less.

"Right. Well, we should be there soon, provided the road stays clear and the storm doesn't worsen before then," Max said.

"So, where did y'all learn to do that? I wouldn't have pegged you for the gung-ho, shoot em up types," Drew asked cautiously. Concern over who their new companions were would not be held at bay. It was one thing bringing Kate back with him—at least she had been honest with him—to a point. They knew nothing about the siblings, other than the fact that they could handle themselves in sticky situations, which could come in handy—but it could also prove to be disastrous for his group. He could very well be putting his friend's lives in danger, and that didn't sit well with him.

"We had to learn—fast. I'd never so much as touched a gun before this, let alone fired one. Max taught me," Megan explained. "He's an Army Ranger...or was...not sure there's an Army left anymore," Megan said, her voice thick with emotion. "After my husband died, followed by our brother, it wasn't long before my daughter and our nephew followed; once that happened we realized we needed to be as prepared as possible. So, we outfitted this truck with whatever weapons and supplies we could find, and we learned from our mistakes."

"I lost my daughter a few weeks back," Kate said softly. "I know what it's like to lose someone you love, to feel helpless, and want to hit back at life in rage."

Drew reached out to squeeze Kate's hand. Whatever blame she held for the situation they faced now, she didn't deserve losing her daughter because of it. No one should suffer the loss of a child. It was a feeling that hit far too close to home for him. After the loss of his niece, Tyson and Violet had given up. Life didn't hold the same joy for them and it had torn them apart.

"I'm truly sorry for your loss, Kate," Max said. "We've all lost someone. Unfortunately, it's a way of life now. But it can't define us. As much as it hurts, we have to survive *for them*, for the one's we've lost. It's the only way we can move forward and try to regain some semblance of an existence."

"How long have you two been out here on your own?" Drew asked, still eager to discover more about their travelling companions.

"Two weeks," Megan said, turning to face Drew. "We were with a larger group for a few weeks. Our camp got overrun and they just didn't have the knowledge to survive. We were forced to flee. We tried to save them, but there were too many of those things."

"We were attacked just outside of Lawrenceburg weeks ago. We had no choice but to scatter. Most of us got separated. My brother was one of those people. I've been searching for him ever since," Drew confessed. He understood the situation they had faced had not been an easy one.

"What makes you think your brother is still alive?" Megan asked.

"I know my brother—he's not going down without a fight, and he has plenty of fight left in him. I just have a gut feeling that he's still out there."

KATE

Kate stared out the window into the darkness. Thinking of her daughter, of Lizzie, always took her breath away. Max had a point though...she had to survive. Not only for Lizzie, but so that she could figure out a way to clean up this mess. There had to be a way, a long-term solution. She just hadn't quite figured out what it was yet. The changes that had affected some people were good for the short term, but she had no idea how long it would last, or even if these people realized what power they had locked within them.

"Hey, you okay?" Drew asked, placing a hand on her shoulder.

"Yes, just thinking," she replied, covering his hand with hers. It was a small gesture, one that gave her comfort. It had been a while since she had felt something—anything.

"We're almost there," Max said.

Kate sat forward, eager to find a safe place to rest for a while. She glanced over at Drew and could tell he was just as eager, though she was sure it was for different reasons. He clearly needed to know his people were safe.

"Take the next right, carry on for half a mile and make a left. The warehouse will be on the right," Drew informed Max.

"Your friends going to be welcoming or should we be concerned?" Max asked.

"As long as you're with me, you have nothing to worry about. Unless you plan on causing trouble, that is?"

"We ain't looking for anything but a chance to survive, buddy," Max retorted.

"Let's just get there in one piece guys," Kate said, eager to dispel the tension that was filling the truck.

"Yeah, cut it out, guys. You can both measure your dicks later," Megan snapped, cuffing her brother around his ear.

Kate chuckled when Max let off a string of curse words in retaliation. The siblings were starting to grow on her. Sobering her up, a bright flash of lightning lit up the night sky. *This storm is nowhere near over. In fact, by the looks of it, this is only the beginning.*

"We're here. Pull up behind that red truck," Drew directed, not waiting for the vehicle to come to a complete stop before hopping out. Making his way around to Kate's door, he helped her out. "Come on, quickly."

They hurriedly followed Drew to the side of the building and waited as he knocked on the door with the butt of his gun. A series of random knocks that appeared well practiced. Drew turned to smile at Kate, and she could tell it was a nervous smile. One that made him even more charming, if that was even possible.

"Damn it! Where is everyone?" Drew muttered. He began backing away, his hand on the hilt of his knife when the door suddenly flung open and he was hauled inside the building.

Without hesitation, Kate went to the doorway after him.

15

Nathan

“W here the hell have you been?” Nathan growled as he hauled Drew into the building. He was damn glad to see his friend, especially considering the events that had unfolded in the last several hours.

"It's a long story, bro," Drew replied, shaking his head. Glancing back, he saw Kate teetering in the doorway. "Come on in, guys."

Three strangers suddenly appeared behind Drew, stepping into the building one by one. The one woman seemed to gravitate towards his friend, while the other two appeared wary as Drew shut and bolted the door behind them.

"Drew?" Nathan's hand automatically reached to take hold of his knife.

"Easy there, Nate. This is Kate, Max, and Megan. I found Kate on the road being chased by a herd. Max and Megan helped us out when we got caught in the storm," Drew explained, placing his hand on Nathan's to stay him.

Nathan hesitantly released his grip on the knife, still unsure of the newcomers, but willing to trust Drew's judgment. Besides, the more muscle they had, the better, considering what was going down. He glanced towards the back of the warehouse, hoping that Shawn had come to his senses and released Connor.

"Where is everyone?" Drew asked, looking around.

"We moved everyone to the safest part of the building to ride out the storm." Taking a deep breath, Nathan sighed. "Drew, we have a bit of a situation."

Nathan indicated to Drew to follow him, leading him away from the newcomers. Once they were out of earshot, Nathan explained the situation to Drew, filling him in on Sully and Julie, as well as the recent run-in with Connor.

"Where's Connor now?" Drew growled, his hands clenched at his side.

"Where I left him—with Shawn…who is currently holding a gun to the jagoff's head." Nathan pointed to the opposite end of the warehouse.

"Take them to the others. I'll deal with this," Drew barked, stalking into the shadows of the building.

Nathan sighed. *It is going to be a long night.* Glancing over at the newcomers he thought to himself, *I wonder if we will ever feel safe around anyone again, or if this is just the way life is going to be from now on?*

"You three—follow me. I'll get you set up in the back with the others while Drew deals with some business."

The three strangers exchanged glances before cautiously following Nathan toward the rear of the building.

As Nathan and the newcomers approached the others, he could hear Julie attempting to calm Maddie.

"You're okay, sweetie. You'll be okay," Julie whispered, holding Maddie close. Julie was sitting next to Sully with Maddie in her arms, rocking her as the poor girl sobbed.

Sully was semi-conscious, aware that something bad had happened, but feeling helpless to do anything about it.

"She okay?" Sully rasped, trying to sit up.

"Sully, stay put," Nathan chastised him.

"What the hell is going on, Nathan?" Sully asked, trying to clear the fog from his brain. "Who the hell are they?"

"Drew's back and he brought some guests," Nathan explained, shrugging his shoulders. "He's gone to help Shawn deal with Connor."

The minute Connor's name was mentioned Maddie began whimpering louder, squeezing herself into an even tighter ball on Julie's lap.

"Hush, sweetheart, you're safe. I promise you, I won't let him anywhere near you ever again. None of us will. Right, guys?" Julie promised, staring Sully and Nathan down.

Nathan hunched down beside the distraught girl. "I swear to you, Maddie. He won't get near you again, sweetheart. I'll kill him before he lays another hand on you."

Maddie uncurled herself slightly to look up at Nathan. Her tear-stained face stared up at him. "Thank you," she whispered, hoarsely.

Sully hadn't been told what was going on, but he wasn't stupid. He must have finally put two and two together as his face filled with rage.

Nathan knew that if Sully ever got his hands on Connor Fitzgerald, he would kill him. Leaning over, Sully gently took Maddie's hand, his heart near to breaking when she flinched at the contact.

"Maddie, darlin', I won't let anything happen to you either. You have my word," Sully said, softly squeezing her hand in reassurance.

Moments later Maddie had finally cried herself to sleep in Julie's arms. Nathan watched as Julie lay down on the sleeping bag beside Sully, turning so that she was between him and the traumatized girl.

"I don't want her to wake up next to a man, she may panic." Julie said quietly.

"Good thinking, sweetheart," Sully whispered back, grasping her hand in his before drifting back into a deep sleep.

Nathan waited silently until Maddie and Sully were asleep before he led the newcomers to the makeshift supply area. He grabbed three of the four spare sleeping bags they had stored and a couple of blankets. Looking around, he realized the only spaces available were either next to Kai or Casey.

Casey Miller was almost as bad as Kai, except she pretended to be nice to you before she would try to stab you in the back. At least Kai was open and honest about the fact that she was a bitch.

"Okay, quick introductions—I'm Nathan, back there was Sully, Julie, and Maddie. These two are Casey and Kai," Nathan said, eager to hurry this along and find out what was happening with Drew and Shawn.

"I'm Max and this is my sister, Megan," the dark-haired man replied.

Stepping forward, the brunette spoke. "And I'm Kate."

"Great, now we're all friendly-like. Max and Megan, why don't you camp out with Kai and Casey. Kate, you can set up near Sully and Julie," Nathan suggested, handing them the sleeping bags and blankets.

"Thank you, Nathan," Kate said, taking hers and walking back to her assigned sleeping place.

"I thought you were going to keep me warm tonight, Nathan-baby—" Kai pouted, bending forward to show off her ample cleavage.

"Watch out for that one. She bites," Nathan spat at Max before storming off to find his friends. That woman was going to go too far one day. God help him, he wouldn't help her if his life depended upon it.

DREW

Drew carefully evaluated the scene in front of him as he approached the two men in the back of the warehouse. Connor was bloody and broken on the ground, while Shawn was crouched over him, weapon drawn and pressed to Connor's temple. The bastard was taunting Shawn, daring him to pull the trigger.

"Shawn—buddy, I need you to put the gun down. We can sort this out another way. No one needs to die today," Drew said calmly, slowly walking up to his friend.

"I can't do that, Drew. Not after what he did to that poor girl." Shawn choked on the words.

"I know, Shawn, and he will pay for what he did. But this isn't the way. We aren't executioners," Drew said firmly.

"How else are we going to stop him? If we let him go, he'll just find another girl to rape," Shawn shouted, his hand beginning to shake.

"We tie him up for now. Keep him that way...away from the others. At least until we figure out a sensible way to deal with him."

Drew crouched down opposite Shawn and slowly placed his hand on the gun.

Shawn looked at Drew, his eyes full of emotion and riddled with pain. Drew knew what Shawn had been through, what had happened to his baby sister. He knew what this must have been doing to him. Yet, even with that, Shawn released his hold on the gun, allowing Drew to take it from him.

"I knew you couldn't do it, you black bastard," Connor spat, coughing up blood.

"Shut up, dickwad," Drew growled, bringing the butt of the gun down on Connor's temple and rendering him unconscious. Drew straightened up and kicked Connor for good measure.

"Drew, I'm sorry—"

"Don't! Don't ever apologize for protecting a woman or a girl from a no-good piece of shit like this," Drew said, stopping him mid apology.

Shawn hung his head. "Glad you're back, man. We missed you."

"Glad to be back, bro," Drew said, grasping Shawn's arm with his hand. He smiled when Shawn returned the gesture. "Now let's get this dirtbag tied up before he wakes up."

Together, they dragged the unconscious Connor to a pillar and tied him up with climbing rope. If there was one thing that got under his skin more than anything, it was abuse of any kind towards women and children.

While Shawn double-checked the knots, Drew stood watching Connor, knife in hand, twirling the tip against his finger. As soon as

Connor woke up, they would make sure he paid for his crimes—one-way or another.

16

Tyson

The truck skidded towards the tree as Violet tried to regain control of the vehicle. Tyson reached over and grabbed for the wheel, turning it as much as he could, hoping to slide past the uprooted tree with minimal damage to them and to the truck.

"Damn it," Tyson shouted, pulling as hard as he could. The wheels regained their grasp on the road's surface just as the front of the vehicle sailed past the tree. Impact was inevitable. Just then, the rear of the vehicle bounced off the side of the tree, sending them into a tailspin. "Hold on!" Tyson shouted.

It seemed like forever before the truck finally came to a complete stop. Tyson exhaled sharply. Looking over at Violet, he checked to make sure she was okay. He could see that she was visibly shaken, but appeared to be uninjured.

"Everyone okay?" he asked, turning to check on their passengers.

"Y—yes" Kelly stammered. "I think so."

"Vi?" Tyson asked, reaching over to stroke her cheek. She hadn't released her grip on the steering wheel yet.

Violet looked at him, eyes wide as she breathed heavily.

"I'm going to drive now, Violet. Slide over," Tyson said, jumping out the vehicle and running around to the driver's side door. "Vi—move, now," he shouted, giving her a gentle shove.

Breaking out of the fog she was in, Violet scooted over as Tyson stepped into the truck. Shutting the door, he cranked the engine. *Nothing.* He tried again. *Still nothing.* *"Damn it,"* he shouted, slamming his fist on the steering wheel.

Outside the window the lightning flashed, as the darkness around them moved. Looking out the driver's side window, he could make out dozens of shadows moving towards them.

Taking a deep breath, he turned the key in the ignition, almost crying out in relief when the engine turned over. Taking his foot off of the brake, he quickly pressed the gas pedal. The truck took off just as the undead reached it.

Kelly was crying, holding onto her father for dear life, while Sam remained silent. Tyson could see that Violet was near breaking point, but he couldn't worry about that right now. He had to get them off the road, somewhere safe, as soon as possible.

"I'm going to try to find somewhere for us to hole up for the rest of the night. We have to get out of this storm before we run out of luck," Tyson said, maneuvering the pickup around a burnt-out bus. "Violet, grab the map and the flashlight in the dash. I need to know where the next exit is."

Pulling out the map, she flicked on the flashlight. Gasping in pain, she dropped the flashlight and map as her body began to seize. Her body was shaking uncontrollably as she fell forward against the dashboard.

"Violet!" Tyson shouted, his concentration torn between the road and his wife. "Damn it! Can one of you check on her, please?"

Sam leaned forward, across the back of the seats and reached for Violet. After finally pulling her back into a sitting position, she quickly checked her pulse.

"Is she okay?" Tyson asked, concern lacing his voice. His knuckles white as his grip of the steering wheel tightened in fear.

"She's got a pulse. It's weak, but it's there," Sam confirmed. "She's burning up though."

"What? Damn it," Tyson swore as a couple of undead stragglers lurched in front of the truck. Unable to avoid them, he hit them dead on. One was sent reeling across the road, while the other bounced as it landed on the hood of their truck. He was face to face with it, the windshield the only barrier between them and the drooling, clawing freak grappling against the glass.

"Get it off," Kelly screamed as Sam was thrown back into her seat.

"Yeah, didn't think of that one," Tyson muttered dryly as he tried to shake the thing off. That was when he saw the exit in the distance. Speeding up, he turned off at the last possible moment, sending the creature flying off into the darkness.

Startling Tyson, the now conscious Duke rasped from the backseat, "You think we're going to get to wherever it is you're taking us in one piece, buddy?"

Glancing in the rear view mirror, he saw the older man rubbing his head as he sat up to hug his daughter. "Trust me, sir, I'm trying."

"Dad! You're okay," Kelly cried.

"I'm fine, sweetheart. Just have a bit of a headache," Duke replied. "What happened?"

"Tyson here saved us from those men who attacked us," Sam explained. "If it weren't for him—"

To Tyson, the possibilities of what might have happened didn't bear thinking about. In truth, Tyson wasn't made for this new world——a world where everyone just took what they wanted without any consequence. It wasn't the way he was raised. And it certainly wasn't the way he wanted to raise his children. Pain struck him as he thought about his daughter. While the pain of losing her was excruciating, great relief filled him in knowing that she wasn't alive to see the world as it was now. That fleeting thought left him riddled with guilt.

"Thank you, Tyson," Duke said, leaning forward to pat him on the shoulder. "How can we ever repay you?"

"By staying alive, sir. And helping me find somewhere to hole up so I can check on my wife," Tyson replied, worriedly glancing over at the still unconscious Violet.

"Of course, son," Duke said. "Where are we?" he asked.

"Somewhere near Decatur," Tyson replied. Reaching over, he scooped up the map from the seat beside him and passed it to Duke. "Any chance you could navigate?"

"Sure thing, son, let me get my bearings," the older man replied, flicking his flashlight on.

Tyson kept glancing over at Violet. *Damn it!* He felt so helpless, but he knew that pulling over without some form of cover would put them all in danger, and Violet wouldn't want that.

"Okay, there's a town coming up...on the right. It's a small town, so we may be lucky and it might not be overrun," Duke suggested.

"I don't think we have much choice. We need to find somewhere safe to check on Violet," Tyson said, looking for the turn. "In the backpack, there are a couple of guns, knives and some ammo for the rifles. Can you reload and make sure we are ready to go when we stop?"

Duke reached for the backpack and the rifles, "Sure thing, son."

Reaching for the gun at his side, he handed it to Duke. "This one too."

Duke took the gun from him and set to work.

Ten minutes later Tyson saw the turn ahead. "Here we go, folks," he said, turning right, and heading towards the town. It appeared quiet with minimal activity, apart from a few undead creeps here and there. Lightning lighting the way, it wasn't long before they were slowly rolling down the streets of what used to be the main street. They had almost reached the end of the street when he saw it. *A medical center.*

"There, that's where we're going," Tyson said, pulling up in front of the building. Turning the engine off, he quickly pocketed the keys. "I'm going to do a preliminary sweep before you guys come in."

"Not on your own, you're not," Sam said. "I'm going with you."

"No way! I can get in and out quicker on my own."

"And if you run into trouble, you'll need someone to have your back. Duke can stay here to keep an eye on your wife and Kelly. I'm more than capable of handling a weapon, Tyson."

"She's your woman," Duke interjected. "Sam is ex-Army, she did two tours in Iraq and knows how to take care of herself. It's the only reason we've survived so long on our own."

"Duke, you know that's not true. We wouldn't be here at all if it weren't for you getting us out of St. Louis," Sam reminded him.

"Okay, fine—but I'm taking point and at the first sign of trouble, we're hauling ass. Got it?" Tyson said, reaching for his gun.

Duke handed the weapon to Tyson, and the other to Sam. "Stay safe, sweetheart." Giving her a quick hug, she and Tyson jumped out and cautiously made their way to the front of the building.

17

Drew

"That should hold him." Drew said, dusting his hands off. Just touching Connor made him feel all kinds of dirty.

"I hope so," Shawn replied, testing the ropes one more time.

"Hey, everything cool?" Nathan asked, walking towards them.

"Yeah, sorry for losing it back there, man."

"Don't worry bout it, Shawn. I wanted to do that and more to the bastard."

"Where's Kate?" Drew asked, looking around for the pretty brunette.

"I told her to bunk down with Sully, Julie, and Maddie," Nathan replied.

"Let's get you some dry clothes, man," Shawn said, putting his arm around Drew's shoulder.

"I'll take first watch on jackass here," Nathan offered before setting himself down across from Connor.

"Thanks, Nathan. I'll relieve you in a couple hours," Shawn said.

"Sounds good."

Drew glanced back at Connor before following Shawn to the rear of the building. He had no idea what they were going to do with him, but there was no way they were going to kill him—there was no way that they could let him stay either.

As soon as he laid his eyes on Kate, he set aside his concerns. She was sitting cross-legged on a sleeping bag, a blanket wrapped around her, drying her long hair with a scrap of cloth. Despite looking bedraggled, frozen and soaked, he was still intensely attracted to her.

"Hey, how you doing?" he asked, sitting beside her.

"I'm better now," Kate smiled, giving his hand a squeeze.

"Head's up," Shawn called out, tossing Drew his pack.

"Thanks, man." Rummaging through his pack for a clean shirt, Drew made quick introductions. "Shawn, this is Kate. Kate, Shawn."

"Nice to meet you, Kate."

"Likewise, Shawn."

"So, what's the plan?" Drew asked, removing his wet shirt, and throwing it to the side. As he picked up the dry t-shirt, he noticed

Kate was watching him intently. He couldn't help but wonder if her thoughts had strayed to their encounter earlier. Just thinking about how close he'd come to burying himself inside of her made him hard—uncomfortably so. Draping the fresh shirt over his lap, he focused his attention on Shawn.

"I don't know," Shawn sighed. "Between Connor, the storms, those things out there, the fact that we need to find somewhere sturdier and safer to hole up—I have no idea which one is more pressing to deal with."

Drew ran a hand through his tousled hair, shivering as drops of cold water ran down his back. Regardless of his erection, he slipped the clean, dry shirt on, relishing in the simple comfort it provided. Thankfully, focusing his thoughts on how to best deal with Connor was enough to eradicate his arousal. *The man couldn't be allowed to remain, and exiling him from the group would be a death sentence. But at least we wouldn't be the ones pulling the trigger.*

Drew finally spoke, "We have to exile Connor. We don't have any other choice."

"I know, you're right." Shawn sighed, "I just have a bad feeling about letting him loose and not being able to keep an eye on him."

"We need to move on, regardless…so, we drop him a few miles out in the opposite direction of where we go. I doubt he'd be able to find us," Drew reassured his friend.

"It might be a good idea to post look-outs on our journey, just in case," Kate chimed in quietly.

Both men nodded in quiet contemplation. Patting her hand, Drew silently thanked her for the suggestion, reassured that she was as concerned with their protection as much as he was.

"Does that mean we're giving up on Ty?" Shawn asked.

"No," Kate replied, grasping Drew's hand in hers. "We won't give up looking for your brother, Drew. Not if I can help it."

He squeezed her hand in gratitude. "I can't stop looking for him, Shawn. But, we need somewhere safe to call home and this place isn't it. I'm not going to risk all of us on the mere hope that Ty will come walking up to the door one day. Once we're all safe we can form small search parties and do this properly."

Shawn reached down and patted Drew on the shoulder. "Get some rest, man, we can talk about this in the morning."

Drew watched as he walked off in the direction of Nathan and Connor. He was concerned for Shawn. His friend seemed to be conflicted over his actions toward Connor and his reasoning behind them. Drew only hoped that he would see that what he had done had been necessary. Where Drew may have been born for this new way of life, Shawn, on the other hand, hadn't. He struggled with everything from the moment the shit hit the fan. Drew could see it, even if others couldn't. His friend never could pull one over on him, and now was no different. Drew would have to keep an eye on him.

"He's right," Kate said, "you should get some rest."

"Thanks, sweetheart."

"For what?"

"Having my back. For not giving up on my brother—or me."

Kate smiled as she leaned towards him. She placed the palm of her hand against his face, cupping his cheek tenderly. "I don't know what it is about you, Drew, but something deep down is drawing me to you. I can't help myself."

Drew tenderly nuzzled her hand, drawing the palm down his face to his mouth. Kissing it, he nibbled at her skin softly, enjoying the way her eyes turned dark with desire and her skin flushed as her body warmed at his touch. Pulling her into his lap so that she was straddling him, he buried his face in her neck, muffling a groan as she shifted closer. Grinding against his straining erection, he thoughts raced. *Damn it, this is not the time, nor the place for me to lose control.* Regardless of how much he wanted to rip her jeans off, spread her shapely legs and bury himself deep in her warmth, he was too much of a gentleman to do it where privacy was an issue. However, before he could say anything, Kate's mouth captured his in a kiss that took his breath away.

The things this woman can do with her tongue—and that is only in my mouth. Heaven only knows what it would feel like to have that warm, wet, silky tongue snake around my cock. The thought alone almost sent Drew over the edge. His control waning, he reluctantly lifted Kate off of his lap and placed her back on the sleeping bag next to him before standing with a certain degree of difficulty.

"I need to check the perimeter. Get some sleep," he muttered before walking away.

KATE

125

Kate sat in shock, her body on fire and her mind racing. Unsure of what she had done wrong, she began to cry. She was frustrated and hurt from his rejection. It was the same story every time; sooner or later she always ended up with a broken heart. At least this time, she hadn't gone as far as to sleep with him. Still she owed him her life and if helping him find his brother redeemed her for their sister's death, it was the least she could do.

"You okay?" a man's voice asked in concern.

Startled, Kate glanced up to find Nathan watching her. She smiled sadly and nodded,

Nathan stepped forward and crouched down beside her, "He's got a lot on his mind."

"I know, I just—" Kate choked up, diverting her eyes.

"Drew's a good guy, don't give up on him," Nathan said, patting her shoulder. "He'll come around."

"How long have you known him?" Kate asked, changing the subject.

"Five years, give or take," Nathan replied, sitting down beside her and stretching out his long legs.

"What did you do…before all of this?"

"Drew and I? We were volunteer fire fighters together, but I mainly worked on bikes for a living. Ty, Drew and I were all into bikes…still are, I guess."

"And Shawn? How do you know him?" Kate asked.

"We crossed paths. He was friends with Drew before all of this went down. He worked homicide, a detective."

"And the other people here, are they all friends of yours?"

Nathan snorted. "No. Apart from Sully, who we knew from before, the others just kinda fell in with us as we went along. So, what did you do before the world ended?"

"I worked for the government," Kate replied, keeping it short and not giving too much away. She didn't know if she could trust Nathan enough to tell him the whole story. Not yet anyway. Considering Drew's initial reaction, it was probably best to wait for a more appropriate time to fill the others in. If that time ever came at all....

"How long have you been here?" Kate asked, changing the subject.

"A few weeks. Seems longer than that at times," Nathan replied. "Hell, not sure if time even matters anymore. At least, not the way it used to."

They sat in silence for a while, both seemingly lost in their own thoughts, when out of no where a loud crashing sound and shouting had them on their feet and running towards the noise. When they arrived they found Shawn unconscious and Drew stumbling to his feet.

"What the hell happened?" Nathan growled, steadying his friend.

"The bastard escaped," Drew spat. "Fitzgerald got away."

18
Tyson

Glancing over his shoulder to make sure Sam was close behind, Tyson cautiously approached the building. Gripping his revolver tightly, he flattened himself against the wall in an effort to get some reprieve from the rain. The elements were against them and the rain was coming down heavy, stinging as the wind whipped it sideways directly at them. With no light, other than the occasional lightning flash, Tyson forced his eyes to adjust to the darkness surrounding them. With a nudge from behind him, Sam pointed to a door a few feet away. Nodding, Tyson moved forward along the wall as quickly and quietly as possible. Just as he reached the door, he prayed momentarily for the coast to be clear before easing it open and stepping inside.

Moving quickly, he edged along the wall with Sam following closely behind him. A sudden lightning flash illuminated the room, allowing him to quickly scan their environment. Weapons at the ready, they both advanced further into the building, pausing only when Tyson heard a scratching noise ahead of them.

Glancing back at Sam, he hesitated briefly before continuing down the hallway. The further they advanced, the louder the scratching became…only now they could now hear moaning noises too. The sounds appeared to be coming from the door at the end of the hallway. Beneath the door, they could make out the slight hint of a light emanating from within. It was faint, but it was there. Gripping the handle, Tyson indicated for Sam to cover him. With a deep breath, his grip on the door handle tightened before finally turning it.

Swinging the door open, Tyson quickly stepped back and raised his gun. Immediately, sharp teeth came at him, chomping, and snapping. Without hesitation, Tyson fired a round straight into the creature's head, the force snapping its head back as it fell to the ground with a thump. Bracing himself, he expected more to follow. When none did, he stepped over the decaying corpse and into the room. The light source they had seen from outside the room was a small camping lantern. Lifting it, he surprised to find it relatively full. It couldn't have been on for long. Given the state of the room and the level of decay on the corpse, he surmised that death must have been within the last couple of days.

Making her way to the corner of the room, Sam began quickly rummaging through the dead one's belongings.

"He has a stash of tinned food and ammo in here."

"That's something. Leave it for now. We need to clear the building and bring the others in," Tyson replied, his voice taut with worry.

"Okay, you take the left side and I'll take the right side?" Sam suggested, picking up the lantern.

"Sounds good. Let's go."

Leaving the room, they moved swiftly down the corridor, clearing each room as they advanced deeper into the building. Having seen little in the way of undead, Tyson allowed himself to hope that they would be able to clear the building without further incident. Unfortunately for them, it was a hope that was short-lived. Opening the last door, he found another corridor—a corridor filled with the undead. Tyson's stomach flipped as he quickly shut the door.

"What is it?" Sam asked, moving towards him.

"Shhh!" Tyson hissed, motioning towards the door.

Edging closer, Sam placed her ear against the door. Without even looking, she knew there was more than one corpse that lay beyond the door.

"Do we have a choice?" she asked softly.

"No. We can't risk leaving them to roam around. We need to do this"

Sam sighed as she placed the lantern on the floor beside the door. Checking her weapon, she took a deep breath and nodded that she was ready.

Gritting his teeth, Tyson braced himself before opening the door again.

The dead came at them the minute they stepped through the door. The sounds of gunfire beat in tune to the gnawing and snarling of the bloodied bodies. Distracted by the room full of creatures, Sam cried out as one snuck up on her. Before Tyson could go to her aide, decomposing fingers grasped his jacket causing him to lose his balance and fall against the wall. He struggled desperately with the creature before sliding to the floor, the creature's jaws snapping dangerously close to his exposed neck. Tyson stared straight into its lifeless eyes. What was reflected back terrified him to his core. The last thing he wanted was to end up as one of them...the lifeless, roaming undead. *No, I can't go out like that—not like this.*

Tyson roared as a wave of energy surged through him. Pushing the creature off, he rolled on top of it and pressed his knee down onto its rotting stomach, holding it in place. Placing the gun to its head, he pulled the trigger, watching unflinchingly as its skull exploded and decayed brain matter sprayed the walls and floor surrounding them. Glancing around, his eyes frantically searched for Sam. Catching sight of her, he was relieved to see she was still standing as she finished off one of the creatures with her knife.

"Did we get them all?" he asked quietly.

"Yeah, looks like it."

Tyson took a deep, relaxing breath and immediately wished he hadn't. The stench of decay and death that assaulted his senses made his eyes water. Gagging, he was thankful that his stomach was too empty for anything to come up.

Walking up to him, Sam placed a gentle hand on his shoulder. "You okay?" she asked.

"Yeah, I just need a minute."

Nodding, Sam left him to collect himself. He watched as Sam checked each corpse to confirm that they were indeed dead. Nothing could have prepared him for this, absolutely nothing. Killing walking corpses hadn't exactly been included in the handbook of life. *This is one hell of a way to live,* he thought to himself.

Finally able to shake himself from the haze, Tyson forced himself to move, walking towards the rear of the hallway. Sam on his heels, they quickly checked the remaining rooms for any further threats. They moved forward in unison, covering one another as they opened the doors, first on the left, then on the right. Once the last room had been cleared they both breathed a sigh of relief. Giving Sam a thumbs up, Tyson smiled weakly.

"Let's go get the others," Tyson said, striding towards the front of the building with Sam following closely, lantern in hand. As Tyson slowly opened the main door, the only sound he could hear was that of the storm. Ever so cautiously, he stepped out into the night and made his way back towards the pickup truck.

Just as they arrived at the truck, Duke's door flung open. "Is it clear?" he asked.

"Yeah, let's move. Quickly," Tyson hissed.

The women grabbed the gear from the truck while Tyson scooped Violet into his arms. Leading the way back to the building, Duke ushered everyone inside before shutting and barring the door behind them.

Once safely inside, Tyson gently placed Violet down behind the reception desk.

Sam gently placed the lantern on the desk and crouched down beside them. "What do you need?" she asked.

"I need her to wake up," Tyson replied as he gripped Violet's hand in his, relieved that they had found a safe place to tend to her.

Sam nodded, awkwardly patting him on the shoulder as she stood to leave.

"Hey," Tyson said.

Stopping, Sam turned to look at him.

"Could you give me a hand?"

"Sure," Sam replied.

Together they worked to examine Violet. Sliding his hands over Violet's body, Tyson checked for any external injuries that would explain her condition. As he gently slid his hands up her back, his heart sank when he felt the warm stickiness oozing from beneath her top.

"Duke, could you come here?" Tyson asked, reaching for the lantern.

The older man knelt opposite them and helped to gently roll Violet onto her side. Tyson lifted her top to see how bad it was, but nothing had prepared him for what he saw. Bile rose in the back of his throat when he saw the lacerations—bloody and pus filled—stretching across Violet's lower back.

"Damn it, son. I'm sorry," Duke said softly.

"There has to be something we can do," Tyson's voice trembled with emotion. "Sam, grab some bandages, antiseptic, antibiotics...hell, just grab everything you can get your hands on."

Sam exchanged a knowing look with Duke before taking a step back.

"Son—" Duke said softly.

"No, don't tell me it's too late. I can't lose her again. I won't!" Tyson interrupted. He knew exactly what Duke was going to say. Deep down, Tyson knew it to be true, but he wasn't about to give up. Not now. Not again. He couldn't fail her. The only thing they had left in this world was to fight for the people that they loved.

"I'm sorry," Duke mumbled.

Jumping up, Tyson grabbed his backpack and rummaged around until he found some antiseptic and bandages. The others watched as he gently applied the ointment, covered the wound with gauze, and with Duke's help, secured it with the bandage. Together they made Violet as comfortable as possible before all four of them sat down to wait for the inevitable.

Drew was furious. *How could he have let Connor get the slip on them like that?* Pacing back and forth, he fumed while Nathan tended to Shawn.

"Damn it!"

"Drew, calm down. He's gone, and right now there's nothing we can do," Nathan snapped. "Help me with Shawn, will ya?"

Unclenching his fists, Drew focused on Shawn, who was bleeding heavily. *Connor really clocked him hard.* Together he and Nathan half carried, half dragged Shawn over toward the rest of the group.

"What happened?" Julie asked. Jumping to her feet, she rushed over to help them.

"That asshole, Connor, got the jump on us," Drew growled as they set Shawn down on Kate's sleeping bag. Stepping back, fists clenched at his side, he watched Kate and Julie attend to Shawn. *Damn it. I was too distracted. It's all Kate's fault. She is getting under my skin and it's going to get me and the people I'm responsible for killed.*

Nathan was watching him, a knowing look on his disheveled face. It was as if his friend knew that he was holding himself responsible, and by the way he was looking at Kate, he felt she was the reason behind it.

"Drew, come with me," Nathan said, grabbing his arm and yanking him off to one side.

"What the hell?" Drew shook his friend's hand off him.

"Cool it, bro," Nathan held his hands up. "If looks could kill, that poor woman would be six feet under and then some by now. It's not her fault Connor got away, and it's not fair to blame her for whatever is going on in that thick head of yours."

Drew took a step back. Nathan may as well have punched him in the gut. Even that would have been less of a shock. He'd never known his friend to be so forthright and defensive.

They stood and stared at each other in silence for a few moments, Nathan's words sinking in the more Drew thought about it. Still, it wouldn't do for him to allow thoughts of Kate to cloud his judgment in the future. *Best I stay as far away from her as possible, for everyone's sake.*

Shawn stirred, mumbling as he fought to regain consciousness. Kate continued to apply pressure to his head, gently holding him down in the process.

"What happened?" Shawn muttered, straining to open his eyes.

"Connor knocked you out," Drew replied. "He escaped."

"Damn it!" Shawn snapped, pushing Kate away and struggling to his feet. The fool was swaying as he tried to walk toward the entrance.

Before Shawn fell over, Nathan grabbed his arm, stabilizing him. "Shit, you shouldn't be walking around right now, dude."

"Get the fuck off me, man! I need to find that bastard before he hurts someone else," Shawn snapped.

"I don't give a fuck about anyone other than you right now, Shawn. If you don't sit down, I'll take you down," Nathan replied calmly while leading their friend back to the sleeping bag.

Drew watched silently, noticing a change in Kate. Stepping forward, he tried to get a closer look. Gasping, he took a step back. Her eyes were glowing yellow in the dimly lit room, while her features appeared sharper and more pronounced. The moment their eyes made contact, she quickly turned away from him.

"What's wrong?" Nathan asked, stepping towards them.

"Nothing," Kate replied quickly. "I think we all just need to take a deep breath, calm down, and think about this logically."

"Calm down? What the fuck? That bastard is out there—"

"Exactly! He's out there…probably getting as far away from us as possible. So, yes, we need to take a beat and calm the fuck down," Kate snapped, keeping her face to the shadows as she inhaled deeply.

Walking up to Kate, Drew hesitantly placed a hand upon her shoulder. She tensed at first before turning to face him, a sad smile playing on her pale face. It took everything he had to resist the urge to pull her into his arms. *Fuck! Why does she have this hold on me? She is the reason we are all in this mess. No, it isn't entirely her fault—but she was involved.* She was a part of it, and that was something Drew couldn't just ignore.

"Kate's right. There's no sense in blaming each other, or ourselves. The bastard is gone and hopefully he'll stay that way," Drew said, squeezing her shoulder.

"Thank you," she said softly. Her eyes met his and for a moment he thought he would disappear into their depths. Shaking his head, certain he was losing his mind, Drew stepped away from Kate and walked over toward Shawn. His priority right now was to ensure that his friend was okay and that everyone under his protection remained safe and alive.

"Buddy, you really do need to rest up. You took one hell of a knock to that thick head of yours," Drew admonished his friend, squatting down beside him.

"This is all on me, Drew. I shouldn't have let him get the slip on me like that. I won't let him get away with it," Shawn babbled, attempting to get up again.

Drew not so gently shoved Shawn back down. Listening to the thunder roar above the sound of the rain, he sighed. *This is going to be one hell of a long night.*

NATHAN

Nathan stared at Kate. She was hiding something, and that didn't sit well with him. Whatever it was, Drew was covering for her—that much was obvious.

Striding toward Kate, he pulled her aside. "What the hell is going on? And don't give me any bullshit about Fitzgerald. That look on your face had nothing to do with him."

Kate inhaled sharply and tried desperately to move away from him. Tightening his grip, he pulled her closer. "Answer me. Now," Nathan hissed.

"I—I can't," she stammered, avoiding eye contact.

Before Nathan could speak a huge crash at the front of the building had him reaching for his gun. Almost instantly, Drew was at his side, weapon drawn.

"What the hell was that?" Drew asked.

"I don't know, but whatever it was, it can't be good," Nathan replied.

"Kate, go watch Shawn," Drew ordered.

As she hurried back to Shawn, Max appeared from the rear of the building.

"Max—come with us, and bring a weapon," Drew called out.

"I'm coming too," Megan said, walking up behind her brother.

"You armed?" Nathan asked, skeptically.

"Damn straight I am," she replied, lifting her shirt to reveal not one, but two guns strapped to her hip.

Nathan nodded. He was unsure whether she knew how to handle herself, but he also realized that they needed the extra hands. Inching forward, he and Drew took the lead, while the siblings brought up the rear.

Nathan was the first to arrive at the front door. Upon his arrival, he was able to see that a beam had dislodged and crashed in front of the door, blocking their only safe exit. It was obvious that it was going to take more manpower than they had available in order to shift it.

"Fuck!" Nathan shouted, kicking at the metal barrier. Bracing his hands against the wall, he took a few deep breaths. He couldn't lose it now. Not when they were down two men and they had a deranged monster out there on the loose, along with all the other monsters. Nathan began to chuckle to himself, unsure which breed of monster was worse.

Nathan could feel himself beginning to unravel. He'd always considered himself a good man—a strong, capable man to have around, but everyone had their limits and his were being tested today. Between Sully's misadventure, discovering what kind of man Connor really was, and now Shawn being laid up—it was no surprise that he was acting a little frayed at the seams. It didn't help that in the last few weeks he had taken on a lot of Drew's responsibilities. Not that he blamed Drew. His friend was understandably preoccupied with trying to find Tyson. However, Drew needed to realize that he was needed here…to lead this group with him. He couldn't be expected to do it all alone.

"Nate—I'm sorry," Drew said, moving to stand next to Nathan.

Nathan looked at him questionably, a frown playing on his brow. "What for?"

"For not being around. I've fucked off and left you to deal with all of this on your own," Drew swept his arm around the room. "It hasn't been fair to expect you to take it all on without my help."

Nathan shook his head and stood up straight. "Drew, you need to find Tyson. I understand that better than anyone. If I could find my sister—"

No one knew better than Drew just how hard it was for him to have given up looking for Claire after their town was swarmed with undead creatures. He had no choice but to abandon the search and get out with the rest of them. Ever since that day, the guilt had been eating at him, and it killed him to know that his sister may still be out there, battling God knows what. The only thought worse than that was that she may not be.

"No, Nate, my priority should be this group. If Ty is alive he's old enough and ugly enough to take care of himself for a while. Once we've found somewhere safer for everyone to hole up then maybe I can start looking again," Drew said firmly, crossing his arms.

Nathan thought about arguing, but he knew Drew well enough to know that he wasn't going to back down. No matter what the best course of action was, he would put the group's well being ahead of his own. Nathan respected that, and yet, it didn't sit well with him that Drew would give up the search for Tyson so easily.

"Fine, we get everyone moved somewhere safe and then one of us will help you look for Tyson," he agreed. Turning to Max and Megan, he said, "You two come with me."

Nathan strode toward the rear of the building with the siblings following closely behind, and Drew on their heels. Stopping at the rear entrance to the warehouse, there was a large, rolling garage type door, which was blocked by various crates. It had obviously seen better days. "We need to get these crates moved at first light. Once they have been shifted, we need to book it. We have two vehicles and not nearly enough room."

"My truck can fit five people...six at a push," Max interrupted.

"Good, that will help," Nathan replied. "We need to gather everything together and be ready to move at first light."

Holding his hands up, Drew interjected. "Nate, it's one thing to say we just up and leave, but where the hell are we going? We need to scout for a safe place to hole up."

"Drew, we have been scouting places—Shawn, Sully, and me. We finally came to a decision about where to go."

"And where's that, Nate?"

"The ocean," Nathan replied calmly, staring Drew dead in the eye. "We head for New Orleans, find a boat and go to one of the new settlement islands that were never populated."

"You're crazy! How the hell are we going to get clear across the country without getting attacked?" Drew asked, running a hand through his tousled hair in frustration.

"The old-fashioned way," Nathan replied calmly. "We drive."

Violet's fever was worsening and she was shaking uncontrollably, moaning, and writhing in pain. They felt so helpless. There was nothing that any of them could do to change the outcome. All they could do was sit, wait, and keep watch over her. Burying his head in his hands, Tyson felt consumed with guilt. Guilt over time wasted away from her and for not realizing sooner that she was everything to him. Now it was too late.

"Son, why don't you get some rest; I can keep an eye on her for a while," Duke suggested softly.

Tyson looked up at the older man and saw the sincerity and kindness in the man's eyes. Still, despite the offer, Tyson knew he wouldn't be able to rest. He couldn't leave her. He wouldn't. "Thanks Duke, but I'm not going anywhere."

Duke nodded in understanding, stood up and joined Kelly and Sam on the other side of the room.

Pulling Violet into his lap, Tyson held her close. Gently stroking her hair, he silently prayed she would open her eyes, if only once more before the inevitable happened.

"Tyson?" Sam returned to his side and knelt beside him. "Do you want one of us to do it...when it's time?"

"No!" he snapped. "No one touches her except for me."

"Okay," she said softly. "We just thought it may not be best if you're the one to do it."

"Thank you, Sam. But this is on me, and I need to be the one to end it for her when the time comes."

Sam nodded before standing.

Tyson was acutely aware of his three companions hovering nearby, each one at hand should he not be able to handle it. He wasn't afraid to pull the trigger; not on the undead. However, he was afraid that once Violet died, he would still consider her 'her' after she came back. Unfortunately, that was something he would have to face when the time came.

"Ty—" Violet mumbled, her eyelids flickering open.

"Violet—sweetheart, I'm here," he said, stroking her cheek.

"It hurts," she groaned.

"I know, but I've got you," Tyson's voice cracked as he fought to hold back the tears.

"Please make it stop," Violet begged, her body shaking even more now.

"I don't know what to do, Vi."

"Please...end it—"

"No!" Tyson cried. "Don't ask me to do that. Not while you're still you."

"Ty, please...I can't take it. I need you to do it."

"Vi—"

"Ty, I love you," she whispered.

Those words were music to his ears. Yet, those same words shattered his heart and world into a million pieces. "I love you too, sweetheart," Tyson said, choking back a sob.

"Promise me you'll do it."

"I promise."

"Grace and I will be waiting for you, Ty," Violet whispered before losing consciousness once again.

Tyson pulled Violet into his arms one last time, inhaling the scent of her skin, feeling her heart beating in time with his. Kissing her tenderly, his lips left their mark on her forehead. The fever had claimed her, and it was time.

"Forgive me, my love," Tyson whispered as he pressed the gun to her temple and pulled the trigger. Grief wracked his body as he watched the blood run down her face, a face that was no longer beautiful. He had lost her for the second and final time. Without hesitation, he lifted the gun to his head.

"Tyson—please put the gun down," Duke asked softly, appearing at his side. "This isn't the way. It's not what she would have wanted."

"You don't know what she wanted. You didn't know her," Tyson cried.

"Tyson—" Kelly knelt beside him and reached for his free hand. "You know dad is right. Violet wouldn't want you to die this way. No one should die this way."

"Please, son, lower the gun," Duke pleaded, his voice quivering with exhaustion and fear. "Think about those you still have left."

Tyson's head cleared slightly and looked at Duke. Seeing the concern and fear in the man's eyes, he heard the truth in what he was saying, giving him cause enough to lower the weapon. Reluctantly, he handed the weapon over to Duke.

"We need to bury her," Tyson said, his voice cracking as he stood up. "At first light. We don't go anywhere until she's been laid to rest."

Sam didn't say a word; she just walked up to him and wiped away the blood spatter on his face and neck with a piece of cloth.

Tyson could barely breathe, let alone move to stop her. He just sat there as she gently dabbed Violet's blood off his skin. He watched helplessly as Duke placed a sheet over Violet's body, the lump in his throat threatening to choke him as he held back the tears.

"Let it out," Sam soothingly advised. She squeezed his shoulder before walking away.

Walking toward the front of the building, Tyson stared at the door. It seemed as if it were only moments ago that he'd broken into that cabin and found himself face to face with the last person he'd ever expected to run into in the middle of a fucking zombie apocalypse, or whatever the hell this was.

It had almost been an entire day since he'd felt her arms around him, her lips on his, the sweetness of her breath against his skin. Those last intimate moments with her would be the ones he would remember. The ones that would offer comfort in the darkest of days and yet, they would also be the memories that would haunt him and make his heart ache with longing.

Reaching for the chair next to him, he picked it up and threw it against the wall. "Fuck!" he screamed. Again, and again he repeated his actions with whatever he could get his hands on until there was nothing left to throw. In those few moments, he'd uttered more swear words than he had in his entire life.

Broken and spent, he fell to his knees amongst the rubble of his anger and wept. He wept for the love of his life and for the end of life as they knew it, he wept for his family, his friends, and lastly for himself. In that moment, he felt complete and utter despair ravage his soul, turning his blood to ice and causing his stomach to lurch. *What the fuck am I going do? If Drew were here, he would know exactly what to do. He would take over and order Tyson around.*

Growing up, Tyson had resented that Drew was the older brother—even if it were only by three minutes. Drew never let him forget that. Now, he would be grateful for his brother's bossiness if it meant he wouldn't have to deal with any decisions right now.

"Son?" Duke whispered, appearing beside him.

"I'm okay," Tyson said. "I'm okay."

"It's all right if you aren't. You have every right to be upset, son." Duke lowered his voice and crouched closer. "Don't tell Kelly, but I had to do the same thing to her mother."

Looking at Duke, Tyson could see his own pain reflected in the older man's eyes. However, he also saw something else. He saw resolve. He saw determination, and he saw a fight in the old man that inspired him.

"I'm truly sorry, Duke."

"It was a few weeks ago now, but Kelly doesn't know. I don't want her to look at me differently for it, ya know?"

Tyson nodded. He could understand and respect that. "Your secret is safe with me," he said honestly.

"Thank you, son. Now, I think we should all try to get some rest before sun-up. Once we've seen to your wife, we need to discuss where we head next. As 'nice' as this place is, it ain't safe in the long run." Duke smiled softly.

"You're right. I'll keep watch while y'all get some shut eye."

"We can take shifts, you need to sleep too."

Before Tyson could argue with Duke, the sound of breaking glass filled the room.

Above the sound of the storm outside, the groans and moans of the undead began echoing through the room, filling each of them with dread.

21

Drew

"Drive? That's your big plan? Drive to New Orleans—" Drew asked, exasperated at Nathan's calmness, considering the perils which awaited them beyond the walls of the building.

"Yes," Nathan replied, crossing his arms in front of him. "We have enough vehicles. We take all the supplies and pick up more along the way. We also have sufficient ammo and weapons to keep us safe on the journey."

"Nate, it's not that simple," Drew argued, running a hand through his hair in frustration.

"Then what do you suggest we do, bro?" Nathan snapped. "Sit here with our asses hanging out, and wait to be killed on a supply run? Or better yet, should we wait for a miracle to happen?"

"I'm not saying that. I'm just suggesting we think this through before we go off half-cocked and get everyone killed...or worse."

"What other option do we have, Drew?" Nathan asked, lowering his voice. "This place ain't gonna hold out much longer, and with Connor out there somewhere, we just can't hang around waiting for the other shoe to drop."

Drew knew he was right. *Damn it! This isn't going to be easy but we do need to relocate...and soon. Hell, if we are going to do it, we may as well find somewhere a bit more permanent with some hope of a future without having to look over our shoulders all the time.*

"He's right, Drew," Kate said softly, stepping out of the shadows. "Few people would have been aware of the settlement off the coast. And even fewer would have even considered it an option."

Taking a step towards Drew, she smiled softly when he remained and allowed her to approach him. "Nathan, can you give us a minute, please?"

"Sure. I'll go check on Sully and Shawn," Nathan said.

"Thank you," Kate replied, flashing him a smile.

"Now is not the time, Kate," Drew warned her.

"When will be a good time, Drew? None of us know how much longer we have. Nothing is guaranteed in this life. Hell, we may all die tomorrow...and then what?" Kate snapped.

"Fine, what do you want to talk about?" Drew shrugged.

"What the hell is going on between us?" Kate asked quietly. "One minute you're all over me and the next you act like you want to kill me."

Drew stared at her. He could see a range of emotions playing across her features. Her eyes were weary, yet burning with such intensity it left him breathless.

"You want me to tell you that you make me crazy? That you're so fucking hot I want to bury myself in you and never leave? That if we were alone, I'd have you naked, beneath me, screaming for release by now? That at the same time, as much as I want to fuck you, I want to fucking kill you too?" Drew growled, closing the distance between them and grabbing her arm. "You are behind all of this and yet, I can't fucking hate you. No, I could never hate you. All I want to do is kiss you senseless."

Kate gasped at his words. Placing her hands on his chest, she leaned towards him as if she were offering herself to him. There was no way he could resist her. Call it a chemical reaction or human nature or just pent up desire, but he needed Kate, and only Kate.

Drew groaned as Kate's hands slid across his chest, his desire reflected in her eyes. Groaning, he pulled her into his arms and captured her lips with his. Deepening the kiss, his tongue parried hers in urgency. Kate moaned as he cupped her ample buttocks, pressing his hardness against her.

Damn, this woman would be the death of him one way or another. Of that he was certain. Another certainty was that she was not a 'wham, bam, thank you, ma'am' kind of gal. And he liked that about her. Deep down, he knew that where she was concerned, once would not be enough to satisfy him...and that scared him. But it also made him realize, that for once, he truly needed another person.

Pulling her behind the boxes, he gently pushed her against the wall. With her back to him, he reached around and cradled her neck with his hand while using the other to unbutton her shirt. As he revealed her neck and shoulders, he bent to kiss her pale skin, nibbling his way up to her ear. His hands slid down to cup her full breasts, while tweaking her already rock-hard nipples through her pale lace bra. Her mewling urged him on as he slid his hands down further to unbutton her jeans. Slipping a hand beneath her panties, he found his way to her wet, waiting pussy.

"Damn, you're so wet," he rasped in her ear. "I could just slide right in you, couldn't I?"

Dipping a finger into her wet hole, he held her tight as she bucked against his now straining erection. "Shhhh," he quieted her. "We don't want an audience, now do we?"

"Drew, please?"

"Please what?" he taunted, dipping in another finger whilst using the palm of his hand to rub her clit.

"I want you in me when I cum," she begged.

"Turn around," Drew ordered, quickly removing his hand.

Unbuttoning his jeans, he kicked them off to the side at the same time Kate removed hers. Grabbing a condom from his pocket, he quickly ripped the wrapper with his teeth. Not wanting to waste time, Kate reached for his cock, stroking it. He inhaled sharply. *If she keeps this up, I won't last much longer.* Pushing her away gently, he slipped on the condom and firmly pressed her against the wall.

Kissing her lips, he effortlessly lifted her legs before wrapping them tightly around his waist, and lowering her onto his cock. He was slow at first, enjoying the gasp of surprise as he filled and stretched her. Biting her lip, Drew stifled a moan as her warmth enveloped him. *Damn, being buried deep inside her feels like coming* home, he thought to himself.

Once fully seated inside her warmth, he slowly began to move, while his mouth devoured hers. His thrusts became more urgent as her body began to buck against him. Moments later, he felt her muscles contract as her release washed over him. She cried out, her moans of pleasure matching his own as he thrust one final time before finding heaven.

KATE

Kate hung on to Drew for dear life as every nerve and fiber of her being felt electrified with pleasure. Never had sex felt this good before. *Damn. If this is what sex should be like then I have been missing out on something special for far too long.*

"You okay?" Drew asked softly, gently easing himself away from her.

She found herself standing up, half naked in the dark and speechless.

"Kate? Did I hurt you?" Drew asked, his voice laced with concern.

"No…" Kate replied softly, wanting to quell any worry he may have over her state of being. "That wasn't anything I'd ever experienced before so I may need a moment."

Drew cupped her face in his hands and forced her to look at him. "Are you fucking kidding me?"

She didn't reply, trying to mask the fear that was building within her.

"Kate, are you telling me you've never orgasmed during sex?"

"I thought I had, but now—now I know I haven't. Not until tonight."

"Damn." Drew pulled her into his arms, enveloping her with strength and dare she hope...love. "Woman, you will always cum when I fuck you. You never have to go without again, you hear me?"

"This wasn't a one-off thing then?" she asked, half afraid of his answer.

"Fuck no. I'm not the kinda guy to sleep with a woman once and throw her aside the next day."

Smiling against his chest, Kate sighed in relief. As strong as she was, this man made her feel weak emotionally. Yet, in some strange way, that made her stronger.

"You belong to me now, Kitten. I won't let anything happen to you. Got it?" he growled.

Her head was telling her this was all happening far too quickly for it to be real, but her heart was telling her that this felt right and to go for it. After all, who really knew if either of them would live long enough to enjoy a normal relationship.

Looking up into his eyes, Kate nodded. Leaning in, Drew kissed her tenderly on the lips before releasing her and collecting their clothes.

Together, they dressed in silence, each aware of the other's presence and that words were not necessary at that moment.

"Ready to face the music, sweetheart?" Drew chuckled, taking her hand in his.

"Oh, do you think everyone knows?" Kate blushed.

"I'm pretty sure they have guessed by now," he laughed.

"Right..." Kate hesitated briefly. "May as well get this over with then."

Draping his arm over her shoulder, Drew guided her back to the group. It didn't matter that she'd only known him for less than a day, Kate could sense that Drew already felt protective of her, despite what she had revealed to him about her involvement in their situation. And despite everything, she was grateful that he was beginning to accept that she wasn't solely responsible for the end of the world.

"Hey, what kept you guys?" Nathan asked with a smirk as they joined him, Sully, Julie, Shawn, and Max.

"Mind your own business, jackass," Drew retorted, playfully punching Nathan's shoulder.

"Whatever. While you two were off canoodling, we've been busy planning our escape. We've got it all mapped out, which roads to take and alternatives if those are blocked. We've figured out who will go in which vehicle and we've estimated that if all goes to plan, it should take us a week, maybe two, to get to New Orleans," Nathan explained.

Kate looked at the map and all the plans Nathan and the others had drawn up before glancing at Drew. Seeing the smile upon his rugged face made her feel something for the first time in a long time…something she was certain she had lost for good—Hope.

Tyson froze. They were trapped. Glancing at Duke he could see his uncertainty reflected back in the man's face. Thinking back, he struggled to remember if they had seen any other exits on their initial search of the building. *Damn, this is not the time to lose my focus. Not when I have three other lives to think about, as well as my own.* Although, considering his current state of mind, Tyson would happily sacrifice himself if it meant the others would be able to escape.

Just then, the sound of more glass breaking spurred him into action. "Sam, did you notice any other way outta here when we checked the place out earlier?"

"I don't think so. Damn...my bad, I should have checked," Sam replied, the defeat evident in her voice.

"Hey, don't do that. None of us have been thinking clearly," Tyson shot back. "Duke, you and Kelly stay with Violet. Sam and I will quickly look for another exit."

"Sure thing, son." Duke pulled out his gun and after a moment's hesitation returned Tyson's to him.

"Thanks, Duke."

"Don't mention it. Just don't do anything stupid."

"I won't. I'm planning on getting us all outta here in one piece."

"Glad to hear it," Duke said, offering his hand to Tyson.

Reaching out, Tyson shook Duke's hand, a look of understanding and acceptance passing between the two men before Tyson followed Sam towards to rear of the building.

Tyson was worried...even more so than usual. *If we don't find another way out of this building, we'll have no other option but to fight our way out the front and face God only knew how many of those drooling, undead freaks in the process*, Tyson nervously thought to himself.

"Did we check the door at the back?" Tyson asked, sweeping the light across the room.

"No. Damn, I missed that one."

"Okay, you open the door and cover me?" Tyson suggested.

"Let's do it," Sam agreed. She waited for Tyson's signal before pulling the door open.

Holding his breath, Tyson expected the worst as he moved through the doorway, Sam following close behind him. Once through the doorway, they found themselves in a long corridor, lights still flickering.

"One of the generators must still have some juice," Tyson whispered as they crept further down the corridor.

"Yeah, doesn't look like it'll last for much longer."

"At least it's something."

"Where the hell is this taking us?" Sam hissed.

"Just stay alert."

"You too," Sam muttered.

Tyson shot her a dirty look. Shaking his head, he refocused on finding an exit.

They quickly came upon another door, this one opening outward. Motioning to Tyson, Sam indicated for him cover her. Nodding, he stepped aside, allowing her to go first. Sending out a prayer to any God that may be listening, Tyson braced himself as she opened the door.

Holding his breath, he expected shadows to jump out at them as they both stepped through the doorway. Thankfully, all that greeted them was rain and gale-force winds. They had made it. Quickly stepping back into the building, they quietly shut the door behind them.

"We have a way out at least. But how the hell do we get to the truck?" Sam asked, rubbing her neck in agitation.

"Let's get the others. You can all wait here and I'll make a break for the truck. You'll have to be ready to move as soon as I come around the corner," Tyson said.

"It's suicide. You won't make it back," Sam argued.

"We don't have a choice, Sam. Did you see any other vehicles out there? At least I know the pickup has over half a tank of gas and some supplies in it."

I could sense Sam's concern, but what other option was there? Either I make a run for the truck or we all die in this place.

"Fine, but you're not going alone. I'll go with you."

"No fucking way! I won't risk it," Tyson hissed. "If anything happens to me, Duke and Kelly are going to need you to get them to safety. Until Duke is feeling stronger, you're the one they are going to have to rely on for protection."

"Fuck!" Sam conceded defeat. "Just be careful, all right? We all need you too."

Tyson smiled sadly at her. "Come on, let's get the others and get this show on the road."

"Are you outta your mind, son?" Duke asked once they'd explained the plan to him and Kelly.

"You know we don't have a choice, Duke. It's that, or we all try to make it on foot and that won't end well either," Tyson said.

"Duke, Tyson can do it. We just need to move. Now! Maybe we can create a distraction so that those creatures are more focused on the building than the truck?" Sam suggested, turning to Tyson.

"Great idea. I'm going to have to be quick either way."

"Son, we're going to have to leave Violet. We won't have time to move her too," Duke said softly.

Tyson hung his head, his fists clenching and unclenching, resisting the urge to argue Duke's logic.

"I'm sorry, Tyson. Duke is right," Sam reasoned, stepping between the men.

"Let's just get this over with," Tyson said, the coldness in his voice matching that of the night.

Gathering their belongings, they waited as Tyson said a final farewell to his wife while Sam set the diversion. Together, they led Duke and Kelly down the corridor to the exit.

"Tyson—"

"Duke—not now, please," Tyson stopped him short. "Just be ready to move."

"We'll be ready," Sam said, drawing her gun and stepping forward.

Tyson made certain his gun was fully loaded before tucking it back in the waistband of his jeans. Arming himself with his hunting knife, he exited the building and shut the door behind him. Battling the wind and the rain, he hurried along the wall to the corner of the building. Dawn was beginning to break, which thankfully lessened the harshness of the darkness they had faced the last few hours.

Peering around the corner, Tyson realized that he would be up against a lot more of those things than he had bargained for. The good thing though was that the truck was only a few feet away and those things were focusing more on the distraction they had rigged inside the building before leaving. He could handle the few that were straggling by the truck.

Knowing that he had minimal time in which to act, Tyson darted from his hiding place and ran straight towards the truck. Knife at the ready, he quickly dispatched two undead creatures and made it to the driver's side door. Almost to safety, he heard the zombie before it reached him. Flinging open the door, he swung around and grappled with the decomposing corpse for a moment before his knife found its mark. Throwing the body to one side, he hopped in the truck, shut the door, and quickly pulled away from the building. Honking once as he came around the corner, he saw the door open, just as they had planned. Within seconds of pulling up, the others piled in the truck and he sped off just as the horde ambled around the side of the building towards them.

"Everyone okay?" he shouted. His adrenaline was pumping as hard as the vein in his forehead. Violet had always joked with him that you could tell when he was under pressure just by watching the vein in his forehead as it pulsated vigorously. The memory of her ribbing him made him smile, and yet, it brought with it a wave of

163

pain. Knowing all he had now were memories was too painful a thought to process when they were all still in danger.

"Where are we going?" Sam asked, holding on to the dash for dear life as the truck bounced around corners as Tyson tried to avoid more of the undead.

"We need to head for the coast. New Orleans. If my brother and friends are still alive, I'm sure that is where they would head. Nathan knew about a settlement on an island, somewhere off the coast. That's where he would take everyone. I'm sure of it," Tyson replied.

"New Orleans? How the hell are we going to make it there with what we have?" Duke queried.

"We'll make it. We have to," Tyson stated, gripping the steering wheel tighter.

"Okay. Duke, we don't have any other choice. No matter where we go, we're either going to run into those creatures or people just as bad," Sam said matter-of-fact.

"She's right, Dad. At least it's something," Kelly said softly. Tyson glanced in the rear-view mirror and saw Duke pull Kelly into his arms. *At least they are still together. And I'll be damned if that is going to change under my watch.*

"New Orleans it is then," Sam confirmed, glancing back at the others.

"Okay, it's going to be a long drive. Y'all need to take turns sleeping and keeping watch while I drive."

"We could take turns driving?" Sam suggested.

"If I get too tired I may take you up on that, but right now, I need to get us out of here," Tyson replied. "I let Violet down, but I promise, I'm not going to let any of you down too."

No one said anything. For once he was grateful for the silence. The reprieve allowed him to concentrate on which direction they needed to head, as well as toss around with possible scenarios of what they might encounter. He liked options; escape plans. Finding a way to survive was now his driving force. And for that, his companions would be grateful in the long run.

Tyson shifted in his seat. *May as well get comfortable, considering the drive that lay ahead of them.* Again, he prayed. He prayed that he could fulfill his promise and get them all to the coast in one piece. Strange, the amount of praying he'd started doing since this whole thing began. His family wasn't exactly the religious type, and now—especially now, he would have thought he'd be cursing all forms of higher powers for what was happening. Instead, he found it provided him with a certain amount of comfort and hope in a world filled with despair and death.

All Tyson knew for sure was that someone, or something, out there was looking out for him and he wasn't about to give up. Not yet. Not until he made sure the others were safe. Then…then he would join his wife and baby girl for eternity.

Connor Fitzgerald hurried along the perimeter of the building, fear fuelling his rage as he ran towards an old apartment building. The wind whipped sheets of water sideways, the force of it cutting into his skin, just as a sheet of glass would. Covering his face with his arms, he tried to protect his eyes. Unfortunately, the relief he felt at reaching the building was short lived when a lone creeper appeared from within the darkened entryway and lurched at him.

Connor wasn't quick enough to draw the gun, allowing the creeper to take him down hard. Struggling, they rolled backwards and forwards until Connor could pull the gun free. Placing it against the creature's head, he pulled the trigger, taking unnecessary satisfaction in the sight of bone and brain matter splattering the floor and wall. Realizing that the sound would probably draw more of the creatures to him, he hurried into the building and up the stairs. Cautiously, he climbed each flight of stairs until he reached the top floor and the very last apartment in the building. Regardless of what may be in that apartment, he needed supplies and shelter. *Damned if he was about to let those bastards be the death of him.* Overcome with rage he kicked in the door and entered the apartment.

Expecting darkness or something dead to greet him, Connor was surprised to find the apartment lit with candles and lanterns. Closing the door behind him, as best he could, Connor began a search of the apartment, room by room. It appeared to be abandoned, which didn't sit well with him. Uneasily he approached the living room only to find it empty too. Confused, he looked around and spotted boxes of food, weapons, ammo, and bottles of water just sitting in the middle of the room. *Either this is my lucky day or I've died and gone to heaven.*

"Drop your gun and get on your knees," a voice ordered from the shadows.

Connor spun around, ready to take someone down, only to find himself at the receiving end of a rifle to the stomach. Doubling over, he heard a crack before the pain in his head registered and he blacked out.

His eyes fluttered open, searing pain forcing them shut instantly. *Damn, I feel like I've been hit by a* semi, he groggily thought to himself. When he finally came to enough, he realized that he couldn't move his arms. Someone had restrained him.

"What the fuck?" he groaned, trying to sit up. He could feel something wet running down his face, something he could only assume was blood.

"Shut up and stay put," the voice ordered.

"Look, I don't know who the hell you think you are, but you'd better let me go before I fucking kill you," Connor snapped.

A figure stepped forward into the light.

Smiling, Connor decided a change in tact was necessary. "How long was I out for?" he asked softly.

The young girl took a step forward, her long blonde hair caressing her bare shoulders as she moved. "A few hours," she replied stonily.

Connor smiled. *It won't take much to charm her*, he thought deviously. She couldn't have been more than eighteen and she seemed to be a sweet young thing. "You mind loosening these ropes a bit, darlin'? They're cutting off my circulation. I'm a doctor, so I kinda need my hands."

"You're a doctor?" the girl asked, surprise evident in her voice. Edging forward slightly, her head cocked to one side as if she were playing the options over in her head.

"Sure am, sweetheart. Now why don't you untie me so we can get better acquainted."

The girl stepped closer, squatting down beside him. He lasciviously gazed at her ample chest, her nipples visible through the thin fabric of her tank top.

"How old are you, sweetheart?" he asked.

"Just turned seventeen—before the world went to shit," she replied.

"Well now, you don't look it. You look about twelve, sweetheart."

"I got my mama's youthful looks. She always looked twenty no matter her real age."

"Where's your mama now?"

"Mama and Papa didn't make it," she said softly. "My older brother went out a couple days ago to look around, but he ain't come back since," she confessed.

"You're all alone?" he asked. Fighting back the elation when she nodded, he said, "I can look after you till your brother comes back if you want, sweetheart?"

The girl moved around him, loosened the rope, and scurried back once his hands were freed.

"What's your name, darlin'?" Connor asked, rubbing the feeling back into his wrists.

"Hayley. Hayley Moore."

"Nice to meet you, Hayley. I'm Connor. Connor Fitzgerald, or Doc, as most people call me," he said with a laugh.

Hayley studied him intensely, her eyes boring holes through him as if she were trying to see into his soul. With her blonde hair, blue eyes, and supple figure, she was the epitome of the 'All American Girl.' He normally wouldn't be attracted to someone of her age, but she looked much younger than she was. Besides, he could just picture Maddie and let nature take its course.

"You got anything to eat, sweetheart?" Connor asked, slowly getting to his feet.

Hayley moved behind the old beaten down couch and nodded.

"Mind fixing me something up?"

"Okay, but you stay right here till I get back." Hayley pulled a handgun from the waistband of her tight jeans and waved it at him in warning.

Taking a step back, Connor held his hands up. "I won't move from this room, sweetheart. I promise."

Hayley tilted her head. Sighing, she returned the gun to her waistband and hurried out of the room, leaving Connor to snoop around.

Before she returned with his food, he managed to scavenge two guns and a couple of boxes of ammo, slipping them into his backpack. He would have taken more but he didn't want to raise her suspicions too quickly. It would be enough to take out at least a couple of those bastards who had separated him from his precious Maddie.

After eating the plate of semi-warm canned beans and sausages, Connor groaned with satisfaction. The portions in the group had been minimal, nothing compared to what he had just eaten. Not for a while at least. Sitting on the couch, he watched Hayley as she pretended to read. It was obvious that she was paying more attention to him than she was to the book.

"You must be a very slow reader, sweetheart," he said with a chuckle.

"Why do you say that?" she snapped back.

"Well, either that's a real interesting page or you're not reading. You haven't turned a page since you picked up that book."

Hayley flushed red with embarrassment and threw the book to one side.

"No need to get upset," Connor smirked.

"You see a lot, don't-cha, 'Doc'?" Hayley sneered.

"You have no idea," he admitted.

"Maybe you should get your things and leave…now that you've had your food."

"I'm not going anywhere, sweetheart. Besides, what kind of man would I be if I left a pretty little thing like you all alone to fend for yourself."

"My brother should be home soon," Hayley reminded him. "And he wouldn't be very happy with me if he found you here."

"I think I can handle your brother," Connor laughed.

"You don't know Nick. He's got a temper."

"So do I, sweetheart," Connor said, his voice hard and cold.

Hayley went pale. Mesmerized, she watched him stand and walk towards her. By the time she realized she should run, it was too late.

Connor grabbed the girl, pulled her from the couch, and pushed her to the floor on her stomach. He smiled as she cried out, attempting to fight him off. Holding her down with his body, he pinned her arms above her head with one hand. With his free hand, he reached beneath her to undo her jeans.

Hayley began to scream. The sound startled him. Even though Maddie had cried, she had never fought him quite like this. He liked it. Reaching for her gun, Connor placed it against her head.

"Shut up or I will shut you up," he threatened.

Instinctively, she stopped screaming, although she continued to fight him. "Please don't. Please stop." Hayley repeated those words over and over as Connor pulled her jeans and underwear down. Pushing her legs apart, he unzipped himself. The whole experience had made him so hard. *If I don't fuck her right now, I may die.*

Reaching down with his free hand, he spread her open and thrust himself deep inside of her.

After spending hours using Hayley for his own satisfaction, he grew tired of her constant sobbing, pleading and fighting. She was grating on his nerves. Turning her over to straddle her, she brought her knee up at just the right moment. The pain of her knee connecting with his balls sent him into a blind rage. It was only after he realized that she was staring at him with lifeless eyes, that he removed his hands from around her throat.

The realization of what he had just done sank in as he hurriedly threw his clothes on. Grabbing as many supplies as he could, he left the apartment. He didn't want to hang around, just in case that brother of hers was real. He would rather face ten undead creatures than one pissed off, revenge-seeking brother.

Just as he was exiting the apartment, Connor heard footsteps on the stairs and managed to duck into an open door just as someone ran past and continued up the next flight of stairs. Quickly and quietly he slipped out of the apartment and made a break for the stairs. Aware that he needed to find somewhere other than this building to hide out, he sighed with relief to find that dawn was breaking.

Taking a left, he headed back in the direction of the warehouse that used to be his home. It would be much easier to scout out the area in the daylight. He would have his revenge on Shawn—one way or another.

24

Julie

While Drew, Nathan, Megan, and Max shifted the boxes, Kate and Julie tended to Shawn and Sully. Maddie was thankfully still asleep, all the excitement having exhausted her. The poor thing had clung on to Julie for dear life when she'd started to get up. Sully softly crooned a calming song and Maddie drifted back into a deep sleep within moments.

Together, Julie and Kate changed Sully's dressings and ensured that he ate and drank some water. Shawn, thankfully, was feeling more lucid and the bump on his head was subsiding.

"Lucky you're a hard-headed son-of-a-bitch, bro," Sully joked, easing himself into a more comfortable position.

"Yeah, for once it's come in handy," Shawn laughed.

"Keep it down, guys," Julie admonished while darting a glance at the sleeping girl next to Sully.

"Sorry, Jules," Sully whispered, his eyes softening as he smiled at her.

Julie blushed. *Damn!* All the man just had to do was look at her with those puppy dog eyes and she was instantly lost in the clear blue of them. She was drowning, and the way she felt in this moment, she didn't want to be saved. She wanted to be lost in him—forever.

Shaking herself from her silly fantasy, Julie finished her food and stood up to stretch her legs.

"We should start getting our stuff together. Dawn will be here before we know it and the guys will want to get going as soon as possible," Kate suggested as she stood up.

"The sooner we get away from here, the better. Especially as far as Maddie's concerned," Julie stated sadly.

"Damn straight," Sully agreed, moving to stand up.

"What the hell do you think you're doing, buster?" Julie hissed, gently pushing him back down to the sleeping bag.

"You need help. So I'm gonna help."

"No way. You're not moving until you absolutely have to. With the doctor gone, I'm not risking your stitches bursting open and there not being anyone around to stitch you back up again," Julie ordered.

Her hands on her hips and stern facial expression resembled that of an irate schoolteacher.

Without meaning to, and unable to control himself, he began to laugh. It started as a slow, soft rumble, which worked its way from deep within his stomach until he couldn't contain it any longer. Once he began to laugh, Shawn soon followed suit, as did Kate. Sully watched the corners of Julie's mouth twitch as she attempted to stand firm and not allow herself to cave in. He winked at her and pulled her down into his arms, gently tickling her sides until she couldn't resist it anymore and began to giggle.

NATHAN

"What the hell is going on with y'all?" Nathan asked, stupefied to find the four of them rolling around in laughter. Now was not the time for fun and games. His confusion only seemed to make them laugh even harder.

Eventually, the laughter drew the others toward them. It was only when Maddie woke up, confused, but with a smile on her face that they realized the laughter was exactly what was needed after all the violence and the drama they had been through recently.

Nathan could only shake his head at the absurdity of the situation, but seeing a smile on Maddie's face softened his heart. *The poor kid needs a break.*

"How are you feeling, sweetheart?" Nathan asked Maddie, squatting down beside her. She immediately looked at Julie, silently seeking approval from the blonde to reply. Julie nodded and gave Nathan a sad smile.

"I—I'm okay, sir. Thank you," Maddie whispered, hugging herself tightly.

Not wanting to scare the girl, he let it slide when she called him sir. Correcting her now would be foolish and heartless. He smiled softly at Maddie. "That's good to hear, little lady. You rest up for a bit longer, ya hear. We'll let you know when it's time to go."

Maddie nodded before lying back down and closing her eyes.

Nathan sighed. *If that bastard ever comes back, I will be first in line to make him pay for what he did to Maddie and to any other little girl that may have come before her.*

KATE

Kate could feel Drew's eyes on her. One look at him and she was awash with desire for him. Motioning to Drew, they moved off to the side. Reaching for her hand, his thumb softly rubbed seductive circles across her palm. Her body tingled in response and she felt her skin grow hot.

"I can't stop thinking about being inside you," Drew whispered as he leaned in closer, his breath against her ear sending shivers through her.

"Now is not the time for this, Mr. Hawkins," Kate admonished. She needed to remain focused on the task at hand—ensuring that they all made it out of here together and in one piece.

"No? How about this?" he replied, tilting his head down to nibble her neck and shoulder.

Kate's entire body was on fire as she felt the strength drain from her limbs. Pulling her into his arms, Drew kissed her. Not just any kiss. This was a toe-curling kiss, which left her wobbly, clearing all thought processes from her mind.

"Would you two cut it out already. Geez," Sully joked from across the room.

Kate broke away from Drew, playfully slapping him on the shoulder as she put a decent amount of distance between them.

Drew laughed, a sexy throaty laugh that made her heart skip a beat. *Damn it. I need to stop acting like a besotted teenager and start acting my age.* Which was not easy to do when you had a guy as drop dead gorgeous as Drew nibbling on you and kissing you as though his life depended on it.

"Drew! Behave!" Kate chastised, unable to stop a smile from playing on her lips despite herself. "We need to go over the plan, a few times at least. We can't risk anything going wrong."

"Nate, Max, Megan—can you guys join us, please?" Drew called out.

"Hey, we need to be a part of this too, bro," Shawn said.

"Yeah, you can't expect things to go as planned if everyone doesn't know the plan," Sully piped in.

"They're right, Drew. We need everyone to be on the same page," Kate agreed.

"Okay. Everyone gather round—Kate's right, we all need to know what is going on and what each person's job is. It's the only way this is going to work."

DREW

Drew tried to clear his head of all thoughts of Kate; her body and that damn sexy smile of hers. It wouldn't do any good to lose focus again. He couldn't allow his judgment to be clouded when he needed to remain sharp and ready for action.

"So, the back exit is now clear. We've shifted all the boxes and crates, ready to make a quick break," Max offered.

"We need to do it in stages. One driver and one group of people at a time," Drew suggested. "We have three vehicles and eleven people. Two vehicles of four and one with three so we are evenly spread out."

"Sounds good, we just need to decide who goes with whom," Shawn said.

"Drew, you should take Kate, Shawn and Casey. I'll take Julie, Sully, and Maddie. Max will take Megan and Kai," Nathan suggested. "Everyone happy with that?"

Drew immediately noticed Max and Megan throwing one another a look. He wouldn't be very happy to be stuck in a vehicle with Kai either, but they weren't going to abandon her just because she was a vindictive bitch. Unless she did something to cause someone extreme harm or if she got someone killed, that is. Right now, though, her words were her only downfall.

"I know it's asking a lot, but we need your help. We can help you in the process, if you still want to find somewhere safe to settle down, that is?" Drew addressed the siblings.

"We said we were in. We haven't changed our minds. We just think it may be better for the kid to come with us. You've seen how hard-core our ride is. She'd be safer with us," Max replied.

Drew knew he was right. "Fine, Julie and Maddie will go with Max and Megan."

"I'm going with them too," Sully interrupted. "I need to go with them."

"No problem, we can fit all three of you in," Megan agreed.

Drew sighed. "Fine, you all go with them. I'll still take Kate and Shawn. Nate, you've got Kai and Casey."

Drew could tell that Nathan was less than happy with the travel arrangements. The last thing he would want to do is get stuck on a road trip with Kai. They didn't have a choice though, and at least Casey would be there to help ease the tension. He liked Casey. She was a sweet woman in her thirties with chestnut-brown hair and emerald-green eyes. Even with the librarian type glasses and the outfits she wore, he could tell she was an attractive woman. She was quite a loner and very introverted though. Never joined in on conversations and wouldn't say boo to a goose. It was good that she was going with Nathan…at least she would be safe with him.

"Okay, vehicle assignments are done. Let's all get to work and pack what we need. If we all work together and get the vehicles loaded one by one, it shouldn't take us more than an hour to get outta here," Nathan said.

"One more thing," Drew interjected. "At the first sign of trouble, whoever is already loaded and in the vehicle should take off and follow through with the plan."

"No way," Shawn argued. "We don't leave anyone behind, no matter what's happening. We stick together and make it out together."

"Shawn, we need to consider the bigger picture here."

"That's what I'm doing, Drew. We can't leave anyone behind. It's just not who we are," Shawn stated. "I couldn't live with myself if it were me."

Drew and Shawn stared at one another in awkward silence for a few moments. Drew knew that Shawn was thinking about what had happened with Tyson and the others.

"Hey, guys—enough. We are all getting out of here. Together. Understood?" Nathan said, putting an end to the discussion.

Drew glanced at him and he nodded towards Maddie who was awake and listening.

"Fine, everyone keeps an eye out and at the first sign of trouble you get out of here, no matter what. Okay?"

"Done. Now let's get our asses into gear and sort this shit out so we can get outta here," Nathan replied with a cheeky grin.

"You heard the man," Drew laughed.

Everyone scattered and began to sort the supplies and for the first time since everything went to hell, Drew saw everyone working together, even Kai and Casey. The sight left him filled with a glimmer of hope that things would work out.

Tyson gripped the steering wheel and leaned forward in his seat. Even though it was getting brighter outside, the cloud cover and torrential rains still hindered his visibility. Every now and then the truck would hit a straggler and he'd swear up a storm as body after body bounced off the vehicle.

"Maybe I should take over for a bit?" Sam suggested, gently placing a hand on his arm.

"I'm good," Tyson shot back. Regret filled him for snapping at Sam. After all, she was just trying to help. "I'm sorry."

"It's okay," Sam replied, squeezing his arm before turning away.

For the next few hours, they drove in silence. The storm was finally beginning to calm and there weren't nearly as many dead on the open roads as there were in the towns and cities. Just when they thought they might be free and clear, a tire blew.

"Shit!" Tyson swore as he struggled to maintain control of the vehicle. When he was finally able to bring the truck to a stop, albeit in the middle of the road, there was a collective sigh of relief. It wasn't like they would be holding up traffic. Glancing around the truck, he asked, "Everyone okay?"

Everyone nodded in unison as Tyson released his grip on the steering wheel. Looking around anxiously, he knew that being out in the open and cornered in a useless vehicle might be the death of them. Just as he reached for the door handle, Sam grabbed his arm. "What are you doing?" Sam hissed.

"Changing the tire so we can get outta here," Tyson replied. "Or would you rather we just hang around and wait to die?"

Sam sighed. "Okay, let's think this through before you go off half-cocked and get yourself killed in the process," Sam snapped.

Tyson was about to argue with her when movement caught his attention from the corner of his eye, convincing him that it was probably a good thing Sam had stopped him when she did.

"Everyone, get down," Tyson growled.

Hunching down, they all remained as still as possible, holding their breath as a horde of undead staggered past the vehicle.

Kelly began to cry and Tyson shushed her. Reaching out, Sam took Kelly's hand in hers and squeezed it gently. Almost immediately, Kelly quieted down. Turning her attention back to Tyson, Sam shot him a dirty look.

"What?" he whispered.

"Shush," she replied, darting a glance out the window. The bulk of the undead had long since passed, bar a few stragglers.

They waited breathlessly until the very last creature had disappeared before they were finally able to relax. Sitting up, Tyson could feel Sam watching him as he hesitantly considered their options.

"If we are going to do this, we do it together. There's no going it alone in this world anymore. Got it?" Sam said, staring Tyson straight in the eye.

"Fine, but we gotta do it quickly. Before the next lot come along," he replied.

Sam nodded. The storm had dissipated and the sun was finally beginning to break through the clouds. Pulling her gun free, she checked the chamber and opened the door.

Tyson followed suit and made his way to the rear of the truck. Hopping onto the back of the pickup, he searched under the canvas for the spare tire, only to find it too was flat.

"Fuck!"

"No good?" Sam asked, climbing up beside him.

"Fucking useless. What the fuck are we going to do now?" Tyson picked the tire up and threw it in a rage.

"Calm down. Losing your temper isn't going to help the situation."

"Calm down? You want me to calm down?" Tyson laughed. "You're out of your mind. You know that, right?"

"I'm not the one having an argument with a lump of rubber and metal," Sam spat before taking a step away.

"We're stuck in the middle of nowhere, with no spare, minimal supplies and no hope of shelter—and you're telling me to calm down?" Tyson jumped over the side of the truck and stalked away. He needed to take a beat. As much as he hated to admit it, Sam was right. He was no use to anyone with his temper flaring and his head all messed up. Violet would have lost it with him by now. She'd have put him in his place in no time. Tyson stopped dead in his tracks at that thought. Clutching his chest, he fell to his knees. The thought of her made him physically ache. He missed Violet so much that he could hardly breath.

Suddenly, a hand appeared on his shoulder. He looked up to find Duke standing at his side. The older man didn't say anything. He didn't have to. He simply offered Tyson silent comfort with his stoic presence.

Tyson struggled to take deep, calming breaths and regain control of everything, bar his heart. The pain there wouldn't subside, and it probably never would.

"Thanks," he mumbled, embarrassed by his vulnerability in front of Duke, a seemingly strong and very much together man.

"Don't mention it," Duke replied. "You just lost someone very close to your heart, son. You need time to grieve. Let Sam and I do some of the heavy lifting for a bit, okay?"

Exhaustion suddenly swept over Tyson and he knew that Duke was right. He would be no use to anyone if he continued to push himself. Nodding, he allowed Duke to help him up and lead him back to the pickup truck.

"What are we going to do?" Sam whispered, concern etched on her face.

"I don't know, Sam," Duke replied. "Either we wait and pray that help comes, or we try to make it on foot. Either way, we will be putting our lives into the hands of fate."

"Haven't we been doing that all along?" Sam said, jumping down to land beside Tyson and Duke.

"I suppose we have. Although, a lot of it was down to our own decisions," Duke said.

"Do you really believe in all that fate and destiny stuff, Duke?"

"Sure. I do think we control our fate and destiny to a certain degree...the universe takes care of the rest," he replied.

"Well, the universe has a sick sense of humor then, if this is the plan it has for us. A world run by undead freaks and the living running for their lives."

"Whatever the reasoning behind it all, Sam, at least we're alive. That can't be said about everyone." He nodded towards Tyson.

Sam hung her head.

Tyson knew that being melancholic and negative about their situation now was not doing anyone any good. Yet he couldn't fault Sam for how she was feeling. And the fact that they were both dancing around the fact that he'd just lost Violet was enough to jolt him into action. "Duke is right. We are luckier than most in that we are still living, breathing, and able to fight for our survival."

"Right, let's find a way to get this truck back on the road," Duke said, striding past Tyson with determination. Sam smiled and followed Duke as he walked up the road. Tyson followed suit. Sam's smile soon faded when Duke stopped and turned to them with a look of dread upon his face. Running to his side, Tyson and Sam took in the scene before them. At the bottom of the hill, blocked by vehicles, was a large horde of undead, milling about aimlessly. Biting back a gasp, Sam grabbed Duke's arm.

Tyson felt a pit of dread invade his stomach. *We will never make it through alive.*

"Come away. Quickly," Duke hissed, pulling Sam back towards the truck.

They ran, quickly and quietly back to the vehicle, fear fighting its way into Tyson's mind as all the possible scenarios played out like a movie in his head. Duke motioned for them to get in the truck, and as soon as they shut the doors, he let out the breath he'd been holding.

"What are we going to do?" Sam asked, her voice as unsteady as her hands.

"I don't know. Dammit," Duke muttered.

"What's going on?" Kelly asked sleepily.

"We just need to get out of here and quickly, sweetheart," Duke replied, attempting to remain calm for his daughter's sake.

"Dad? What's wrong?" Kelly cried out.

"Kel, keep it down, please?" Sam snapped. Her patience with her girlfriend seemed to be wearing thin.

"Just tell me what's going on?" Kelly whined.

"A horde—over the hill. They're blocked off by cars for now, but they will break through eventually," Duke explained. "We need to get out of here now"

"How? We can't go anywhere on a flat tire, Duke," Sam said, glancing at Tyson.

"We are going to have make a run for it," Tyson said grimly, pulling himself together.

"Go out there—without protection? Again? No, I'd rather die," Kelly cried.

"You damn well will die if we stay here and wait for the next swarm of those creatures to descend upon us," Tyson said coldly.

Sam flashed him a look that could kill. "Don't scare her, Tyson!" she chastised. "She's scared enough as it is."

"And no one else is? We're all scared. Doesn't mean she needs to make a production of it," Tyson replied, grabbing his backpack.

This entire situation was out of control. They wouldn't fare any better out there than they would by staying put, but it could at least give them a chance of survival.

"Everyone, grab your things," Duke said. "We go now."

A few brief minutes later, laden with supplies, they abandoned the truck and made their way back to the previous intersection. Moving swiftly, the four of them chose a new path and continued on in hopes of something…anything being their saving grace.

26
Nathan

"It's time," Nathan said, standing in front of the door and nodding to Drew. They needed to make a move now that sunrise was almost upon them. Moving to the side of the door, Drew cocked his gun. Nathan glanced back at the others all huddled together in their assigned groups, ready to move on Nathan's word.

"Get the door, Nate. I'll cover you," Drew said.

"Right, you lot, we're gonna check to make sure the coast is clear and then we all move. Together and quickly," Nate barked.

A collective murmur of agreement was all the motivation he needed to force the door open and step out into morning air. With

Drew following closely behind, he made his way around the side of the building. The vehicles were lined up down the side of the building, all but one, which was parked out front, surrounded by undead creatures.

"We can roll the other cars forward one by one and load 'em up. That one will have to wait till last," Nathan whispered.

"We can't fit all the supplies in the other vehicles," Drew hissed.

"No—not unless someone gives up their place," Nate sighed.

"Fuck."

"We need to do this now. Quickly and quietly." Gripping Drew's arm, Nathan shoved him back towards the first car.

With Megan and Kate keeping a lookout, they loaded the vehicles with as much as possible, leaving just enough room for the passengers. They were preparing themselves, ready to make a run for the last truck when gunfire rained down upon them.

"Everyone in the trucks. Now!" Nathan yelled, ducking behind a dumpster. He tried to focus on figuring out where the shots were coming from, but the sound of bullets ricocheting off the walls echoed and rebounded, leaving him no closer to narrowing down the source. They had to go. Pulling his gun, he made a run for the trucks.

Max, Megan, Julie, Maddie, and Sully were already safely ensconced in the sibling's truck, so Drew waved them off. Max didn't even hesitate, quickly driving away. Nathan was relieved to see them drive off without incident.

"Nate—hurry!" Kate screamed as she and Drew helped Shawn hobble to the remaining vehicle. He sped up, knowing full well a bullet could hit him at any moment. It was only when Kate began screaming, and Drew reached out to grab Shawn that Nathan realized the bullets had found their intended target. *Connor. The bastard.*

"Kate, Casey, get in the truck. Now," Nathan ordered, falling to his knees next to Shawn and Drew. "Shawn...buddy, come on. We got you."

Shawn reached up and gripped his hand. "No, it's too late," he rasped.

Looking down, Nathan realized he was right. Shawn had been shot...and it was bad. He didn't have to look close to know that without surgery, Shawn would have little to no chance of surviving. Rage and anguish battled each other as they raged through him.

"Shawn—"

The gunfire had ceased only to be replaced by the growling and moaning of the undead drawn in their direction.

"Nate, we gotta go." Drew placed his hand on Shawn's chest and their eyes met in understanding.

"I'm so sorry, Shawn."

"Go, get the others to safety."

"No one is going anywhere," Kai said from behind them.

Drew looked up to see her pointing a gun at them. Nate reached for his gun, stopping only when she aimed directly at him.

"Uh uh," Kai admonished, waving the gun at them. "Get up, all of you."

Together, Nathan and Drew helped Shawn to his feet. They stood and faced her as a trio one last time. Conscious of the undead ambling in their direction, Nathan knew they had little time left in which to escape unharmed.

"Remember that bar fight at Tanner's Tavern?" Shawn asked as he loosened his grip on Nathan's shoulder.

"No way, you can't be serious?" Drew replied, knowing exactly what Shawn intended to do.

"Fuck it, I'm dead anyway," Shawn laughed dryly.

"Shut up and get back in the building," Kai screamed at them.

"One. Two. Three," Shawn pushed away from his friends and threw himself at Kai with every ounce of energy he could muster.

"Get in the truck!" Drew shouted, running around to the driver's seat. He was already putting the truck into gear by the time Nathan had shut his door. Throwing a quick glance at Kate, Drew nodded to let her know that he was okay before slamming on the gas. The wheels spun as the truck shot forward.

KATE

Kate turned to look through the rear window as they drove away. She watched in horror as Kai shoved Shawn away from her and shut the door to the warehouse. He collapsed and within seconds was being torn apart by dozens of flesh-hungry creatures. The image of those creatures pulling Shawn's innards from his body would never be erased from her memory. It was only when she righted herself in her seat that she realized she was crying. Casey was sobbing, her legs pulled to her chest, arms wrapped tightly around them.

"You guys okay?" Nathan asked, glancing back at them.

Kate nodded, unable to speak.

"Casey?"

"Y–ye—yeah," Casey replied, furiously wiping the tears from her eyes.

Kate reached out and squeezed Casey's hand in reassurance. Catching Drew's eye in the rear-view mirror, she smiled weakly.

"Damn Fitzgerald," Drew snapped, slamming his fist on the steering wheel.

"There's nothing we can do about it now," Nathan said plainly. "We gotta move on and focus on getting the rest of us to safety now."

Kate watched Drew's knuckles turn white as he gripped the steering wheel tightly. She could see the frustration on his face. Again, their eyes met. Only this time she could see the raw pain reflected in his.

"Nate's right," Kate said, grabbing the seat in front to steady herself as Drew swerved to avoid a broken tree limb. "We have to focus on what's important right now."

"And Shawn wasn't important?" Drew asked, angrily.

"I'm not saying that, Drew. Shawn seemed like a good guy, and he died to save us. We can't let that be for nothing."

"He was a good guy; one of the best. He saved our asses more times than I can count. Not just today. What he did...I'll never forget it," Drew replied.

"I know. I don't think any of us will forget. I certainly won't," Kate said, leaning forward to place her hand on Drew's shoulder.

She could feel the tension and anger radiating from him and it worried her. They all needed to remain calm and level headed, now more than ever. Out here in the open, with no shelter, where anything could happen—well, it was a recipe for disaster if just one person's head wasn't in the game.

"We need to keep it together and get to New Orleans in one piece. Once we make it to the island settlement, we can mourn the people we've lost. Until then, we use that grief as anger to get us through this," Nathan said, taking everyone by surprise.

"When did you become all logical and shit?" Drew laughed dryly.

"Well, someone had to be the grownup while you were out looking for Ty," Nate retorted.

At the mention of his brother's name, Kate watched Drew tense up even more. This man had lost so much, and it hurt knowing that she was partially responsible for all this crap happening to them.

If only I'd listened to my conscience and stood my ground when the initial experiment had been suggested. If only I'd gone to my friend in the media when I realized that there was the possibility of something extreme happening. If only... she thought silently.

Kate shook her head to clear the thoughts. She could sit here and ponder the *'what if's'* till the cows came home, but it wouldn't do anyone any good right now. Now was the time for solutions to their problems. The here and now, not what had happened ages ago in that lab.

She gazed out the window, watching the world go by—a world of death and destruction, violence, and fear, the unknown and the reality. The world she saw now was one she didn't recognize. Life before had been about the day to day; planning her next vacation, browsing at her local bookstore, sipping a caramel latte at an overly franchised coffee shop. Life now…well, it was still about the day to day, but now that meant surviving long enough to see the next day.

What she knew could change that and help secure a better future for all of them. Unfortunately, that also meant telling Drew everything—and explaining it all to Nathan too.

Glancing over at Nathan, she could see him watching her. He knew something was up. They had never finished the conversation they had started back at the warehouse. The deep knot in her stomach reminded her that time was running out and she didn't have any other choice. It was now or never.

Taking a deep breath she finally spoke. "There's something I need to tell you guys," she said reluctantly. "And you're not going to like it."

27

Connor

Connor made his way to the building across from the abandoned warehouse without further incident. Climbing the stairs to the roof, he set up camp. *Those bastards have to leave eventually, and I'll be ready when they do,* he thought to himself.

He'd just spent the better part of the last two hours evading the brother of that girl. *There is no way he'll be able to find me* here, Connor thought, laughing to himself. *Even if he did, I'd just kill the bastard.*

Setting up his guns, Connor placed them in a spot that covered both the front and side entrances. No one had ever used the side door, but he didn't put it past them to try and sneak out. As soon as it was light, that's when they were most likely to make a move.

They must have thought he was stupid, but all those weeks he spent with those self-righteous pricks, he spent his time observing them and their habits. He knew them. *Once the men are out of the way, the women will be mine, especially my beautiful Maddie*, he thought deviously.

It was fortuitous that the end of the old world had killed off his wife and her over-protective brother, leaving him as the sole guardian of his thirteen-year old stepdaughter. He'd had urges before, though he had never acted on them. Not while his wife was alive. He wasn't stupid. Marrying a younger woman had eased the urges for a while, but it wasn't enough. Instead, he'd satisfied himself with photos and extra-long cuddles. Once he'd gained Maddie's trust, he knew it was only a matter of time before he'd be able to take it further.

Connor smiled, remembering the first time he'd consummated his love with Maddie. He had to gag her to keep her quiet, which had turned him on even more.

She was his special little girl, and he wanted her back. And what Connor Fitzgerald wanted, Connor Fitzgerald got.

Scoping the building out again, satisfied that there was no movement, he closed his eyes and waited.

A few hours later, the sound of car doors woke Connor. Grabbing one of the guns, he watched them move the trucks around to the side entrance where they loaded supplies. A few moments later, he watched as Maddie ran to one of the vehicles. They were taking his beautiful little girl away from him. Rage consumed him.

As soon as Shawn emerged from the building, he knew he had to kill him. Pulling the trigger, Connor fired shot after shot. He watched, elated, as Shawn went down. Unfortunately for him, he was so intent on shooting Shawn that he didn't notice the other vehicle leave with Maddie until it was too late.

Angry, Connor watched as the dead swarmed Shawn and his bastard friends below. He swore they were done for. His elation soon faded as he watched Shawn launch himself away from the others, distracting the dead so that the living could escape.

The only satisfaction he had now was watching as the dead fell upon Shawn, ripping, chomping, slashing and pulling him in different directions until there was nothing left of him but a bloody pulp.

The others are gone. Maddie is gone. I have nothing left. Nothing. Standing, he dropped the gun and looked down at the dead things milling around, scrounging for scraps of their recent breakfast.

"Why did you do that to my sister," a voice asked from behind him.

Connor started laughing. *Of course, this is perfect.*

"You think that's funny, you fucking bastard?" the voice asked angrily. "You raped her and then killed her. My sister—"

Connor turned to confront his accuser with a smile on his face. "She was a fine piece of ass."

Before he could say anything else, the guy grabbed him and they struggled briefly before the stranger began punching him. Suddenly, the world went black.

A few hours later, Connor regained consciousness, only to find his hands and legs restrained and his head pounding.

"Why don't you just get on with it and kill me already?" he spat.

"We haven't been properly introduced. I'm Nick. Hayley is my sister—or was my sister. She was all the family I had left and you took her from me," Nick said, his voice wrought with emotion.

"Cry me a river, buddy. Everyone dies in this world. One way or another, everyone dies. I did you a favor. One less mouth to feed."

Nick didn't say a word; his fists did all his talking for him.

Connor laughed, blood spraying from his mouth as he spit out a tooth.

"Is that all ya got?" he taunted.

"Oh, I've got a hell of a lot more. And seeing how there ain't no justice in this world no more, I can do what I want to you. Same as you did to Hayley."

Connor watched as Nick pulled out a knife and knelt down next to him. "I'm going to enjoy taking my time with you, asshole." Nick smiled.

SLICE! Connor's flesh was laid open with each new cut. After the seventh cut, he finally passed out from the pain.

When Connor finally woke, he struggled to remember his own name through the excruciating pain. Feeling the warmth pooling between his legs, he struggled to sit up. Looking down, his stomach rolled at the sight. This bastard was sitting in front of him, knife in one hand and Connor's dismembered manhood in the other.

"You fucking prick. What the fuck did you do?" he screamed.

"Did you honestly think I was going to let you keep the weapon you used against my sister? The weapon that you defiled her with?" Nick asked, standing up.

Connor watched in horror as he walked to the edge of the building and let the severed appendage fall.

"You're next asshole," Nick said, walking towards him.

Connor struggled, but he was too weak from blood loss. Nick was too strong, and too determined to be fought off.

Forced to hobble to the edge of the roof, Connor looked down to find the undead milling around on the ground below. Attempting to back away, Nick laughed as he pushed him forward a little further.

"One shove and you'll be flying. You won't last two seconds before they eat you alive—if the fall doesn't kill you first. You messed with the wrong girl, asshole," Nick said. Turning Connor to face him, he closed in on his face before whispering, "I want to see your face when you die."

"Oh, you will, you fucking prick," Connor spat. Grabbing hold of Nick's belt with his fingers, he launched them both off the building.

The expression on Nick's face was priceless, enough to give Connor one last moment of satisfaction before the ground rushed up to meet them.

The pain from landing was unlike anything Connor had ever felt before. That is, until the dead descended on him, sinking their teeth into his already bloodied and mutilated flesh.

He screamed in agony as pieces of his flesh were torn from his body. Connor's final image before death embraced him and hell welcomed him was a half-decayed, oozing face ripping his throat out.

"Maddie…." he gurgled with every ounce of energy he had left.

28

Tyson

The wind howled as it battered the cold rain against the bedraggled quartet. Hours of trudging down the desolate, devastated highway had left them all weary and on edge.

"We need to get off this road," Sam shouted, readjusting the pack on her back.

"If we cut through the woods, we can make it to the interstate a lot quicker," Duke suggested, taking a quick swig of water.

Tyson stopped, dropped his pack, and reached for the water bottle Duke held out to him. The water felt like heaven to his parched throat. Hours of walking, with no rest after the last few days were beginning to catch up to him. He needed sleep, but every time he closed his eyes, he saw Violet. Even when he blinked…she was there. He knew he wouldn't be able to sleep for a long time, if ever again, but he was even more determined to get the others to safety now. The sooner he found them somewhere to hole up, the sooner he could be with his family.

"Tyson?" Sam nudged him for an answer.

"Yeah," he picked his pack up and slung it over his shoulder. "The sooner we get where we need to be, the better."

Without hesitating, Tyson took off up the slightly muddy incline and stepped into the woods. Glancing back, he ensured that the others were behind him before he forged ahead. Thankfully, the trees provided some shelter from the rain, not much, but it was better than nothing.

"Ty—wait up," Sam called out.

He stopped and waited for them to catch up to him, unapologetic about the pace he was setting. Something was driving him, some unknown force pushing him to get them to the road. The only thing Tyson could be certain of was that each step brought him closer to his family, to happiness, and to a way out of this godforsaken world that had destroyed everything he loved.

"Can we take a beat?" Sam asked, grabbing his arm before he could take off again.

"You want us to what? Find a hotel? Roast marshmallows on an open campfire? Grab some rays?" Tyson snapped sarcastically.

"Whoa there, son," Duke said calmly, stepping between them. "No need for that. We're all tired and in need of a break."

Tyson took a step back and an even deeper breath. He couldn't afford to lose his cool, as much as he may want to. "Fine. Ten minutes."

Exhausted, Kelly sat down and leaned back against a tree. Tyson watched as Sam leaned down and kissed her on the cheek. The two women smiled sadly at one another before Sam stood up and walked over to Duke.

The wind raged around them, bringing with it the smell of death. There were undead nearby, Tyson could smell it. The longer they stayed, the more they risked their lives.

"Drink," Duke told Tyson, handing him a bottle of water.

Tyson took the bottle but didn't drink. They needed to use their supplies sparingly. God only knew when they would be able to restock.

"What do we do when we get to the road?" Kelly asked.

"We try and find a ride," Tyson replied. Stuffing the bottle of water into his pack, he slipped the pack onto his back. "We should get going," Tyson said before forging ahead.

The others were lagging, and it was becoming increasingly obvious that the trees were offering less coverage than before. As they continued their trek through the woods, the storm continued raging around them, a crescendo of thunder, wind, and rain.

From out of nowhere, lightning struck a nearby tree, sending it toppling in their direction. Thankfully, Tyson managed to jump out of the way just in time. Unfortunately, Kelly wasn't as lucky.

Kelly!" Duke cried out, running to her side. He may have been in his sixties but he was still spry for an older guy. Though no matter how great a shape he was in, there were still limits to his strength.

Duke tried desperately to lift the tree, all the while, Kelly was screaming in pain. It was no use. It wouldn't budge.

Running to Kelly's side, Sam tried to help Duke lift the tree. "It's too fucking heavy," she yelled, banging her fists on the damaged bark.

Making his way back toward the group, Tyson jumped over the broken tree and pushed Sam out of the way. "Grab her arms."

Positioning herself at Kelly's head, Sam grabbed her under her arms, and watched as Tyson and Duke struggled with the tree. Time seemed to stand still as they worked quickly to free Kelly.

Sam was consoling Kelly, trying to soothe her, and calm her down when hell descended upon them. The storm had masked the sounds of the dead, so they didn't hear them until it was too late. It was only when a cold, decaying hand clawed at Sam's clothes that they realized they weren't alone.

Shoving the creature away from Sam, Tyson watched as it stumbled and fell, knocking three more to the ground. It resembled some sort of a gory themed version of bowling. It would have been almost comical if it weren't so terrifying.

"Tyson, look out," Duke yelled, drawing his attention back to the reality surrounding them. There were at least twenty of the bastards drooling, clawing, and snapping their way towards them; one of them a whole hell of a lot closer than the others. Tyson quickly unsheathed his knife and swung it at the creature that was trying to take a chunk out of him. The knife glanced off of its rotting flesh twice before finally finding its mark through the base of its skull.

Taking stock of the situation at hand, Tyson soon realized that they were outnumbered. Kelly was still trapped and unable to defend herself, while Duke and Sam were on either side of her, protecting the woman they loved.

Killing three more of the already mutilated corpses, Tyson managed to maneuver back to his friend's aide.

Attempting to lift the tree once again, while still fighting off the dead, their strength was waning. They wouldn't last much longer. With no other options, Tyson pulled his gun, praying that the storm would cover the noise. He began firing shot after shot at the creatures as they crept closer. His elation at the accuracy of his shots was short lived as another wave of decomposing, mangled bodies appeared through the trees.

"Fuck, there are too many of them," he shouted.

"We have to get Kelly out," Sam yelled back, firing at the creatures.

"Please, don't leave me," Kelly sobbed.

Tyson watched as Duke attempted to move the fallen tree once again. It was no use. The damn thing was too heavy. Besides, even if they did manage to free her, no one knew what kind of damage had been done. While Duke continued to made an effort to lift the tree, Tyson and Sam ventured to keep the creatures at bay for as long as possible, alternating between knives and guns.

Unfortunately, all they were achieving was attracting more of them than they could handle. Within seconds the decision to save Kelly was taken out of their hands when a ragged, rotting corpse lurched past them and descended upon Kelly.

Tyson and Sam couldn't get to her fast enough and were forced to scramble over the tree. They watched as Kelly screamed for help just before her throat was ripped out. Reacting as any father would, Duke stabbed the creature feasting on his daughter, but it was too late. There were too many of them.

Stumbling back in horror, Duke fell over the tree, but was soon hauled to his feet by Tyson and Sam.

"We have to go. Now," Tyson urged, knowing that their best chance for survival would be to make a break for it while the dead were distracted with fresh food.

"Now!" Tyson yelled, getting in their faces to get their attention. He needed to get them moving.

Sam was the first to rouse. Taking hold of Duke's hand, she yanked him away. Covering them as they ran, Tyson kept an eye out for any surprises.

Running against the wind, the rain beating against them, they dodged broken branches and decaying carcasses. They were exhausted, but they continued to run until they weren't sure if they could run anymore.

Just when they were about to give up they emerged from a clearing in the woods, which led out onto the road. Tyson wasn't sure which way to go; he just knew that they couldn't afford to stay still for too much longer.

"Duke—I'm sorry," he said, awkwardly patting the older man on the shoulder.

Duke just stood staring straight ahead, breathing heavily, his shoulders shaking.

Tyson moved to offer him support only to find the older man stifling laughter.

"You okay?" he asked in confusion.

"Yeah, looks like we may get a ride after all."

Tyson and Sam looked up to see what Duke was talking about. There, in the distance, they could see two vehicles approaching.

Shooting one another a look, Sam finally spoke. "We don't know who these people are."

"No," Duke replied, "but we do know what's back there; what could come for us when we least expect it. I'd rather take a chance on the people in those vehicles than those fucking things that killed my daughter."

Tyson couldn't say anything. Knowing how hard it was to lose his daughter and then his wife, there were no words that could comfort Duke right now. Hell, there weren't any that could comfort him, never mind anyone else.

As if the dam finally burst, Sam began to cry, but neither man could muster the energy to console her.

Loading his gun, Tyson placed it in the waistband of his jeans for easy access before he turned around and walked out into the middle of the road and began flagging down the approaching vehicles.

He only hoped and prayed that they stopped. More importantly, that they didn't end up dead once they did.

29
Julie

Max sped away from the others without a backward glance, and Julie could see that his instincts had kicked in. That getting them out of there as quickly as possible was the only option for survival.

"Do you see them?" Sully asked weakly. "Are they behind us?"

"I can't see anything," Julie replied, turning to look out the back window.

Sully was slumped against her with Maddie sobbing on her other side.

"We need to slow down or park up ahead somewhere so they can catch up to us," Sully said, coughing at the effort.

"No way. We can't risk it," Max replied.

"Max is right, we can't stop," Megan agreed. "We need to be smart about this."

"We can't just abandon the others," Sully said, trying to sit up. "We have to go back for them."

"Drew told me to get us outta there, so that's what I'm doing. I'm not about to go back and risk getting us all killed," Max replied.

Julie saw him glance over at his sister and she nodded.

"Damn it! Let me out," Sully shouted. "I have to go back for them."

"Sully, calm down. You're scaring Maddie," Julie chastised, pulling the young girl close and hugging her.

Sully winced. The girl's crying was getting to him. The guilt was written all over his haggard face.

"I'm sorry, sweetheart. Please forgive me," Sully said softly. "I'm just worried about the others."

Maddie whimpered in response.

"We keep going. Drew and Nathan know where we are going. We're prepared and we have a plan. We stick to it," Max said.

They drove in silence for a while, apart from Maddie's gentle whimpers every now and again. As they drove, Max managed to expertly avoid a pack of dead things lurching across the road, only taking out a few of them. Their bodies ricocheted off the truck at various points, while one landed on the hood, blood and ooze spraying over the windshield upon impact.

It took ages for the windshield wipers and the rain to clear enough of the muck away for Max to have a clear view of the road. As they continued to drive, it seemed the further away from the city they went, the worse the storm seemed to be getting.

"Hey, you okay?" Megan asked him, placing a hand on his.

He exhaled and eased his grip on the steering wheel. "Yeah, I'm good, sis. I got this," he reassured her, easing up on the gas.

In the backseat, Maddie was in shock and Julie was at a loss for what to do other than to hold the child and stroke her hair. As calming as it was to the child, it seemed to also be calming to Julie's nerves too. Having Sully so close to her, his head resting on her shoulder, didn't hurt either.

Considering the situation they were in, she shouldn't have been having the thoughts she was having, but it was unavoidable. Feeling her face go red, she was grateful that no one could see her.

Thinking back on the previous few days she was quite surprised that she was still alive. She was a long way from her small-town library and quiet life she'd led before the world had been turned upside down. That day in the mall, when Sully had rescued her, was the first day she had ventured out from her hiding spot to scavenge for supplies. She'd known that the chances of her surviving on her own were slim, but she wasn't the kind of person to go down without a fight. The only good thing to come out of that whole experience was managing to kick one of those bastards in the nuts before she'd been tied up.

"Julie—" a little voice broke into her thoughts.

"What is it, honey?"

"I need to go to the bathroom," Maddie whispered.

"Oh, sweetie, I don't know if we can stop."

"What's wrong?" Megan asked, turning to look at them.

"We need a bathroom break," Julie said softly, trying not to wake Sully.

"No way! We aren't stopping," Max said.

"We don't have a choice," Julie replied.

"She's going to have to hold it."

"For how long, Max?" Julie snapped.

"Another couple of hours. At least."

"Julie, it hurts," Maddie cried.

"Pull over. Now!" Julie ordered.

"No, I'm not stopping."

"Max, we can't let the poor girl suffer. I think she's been through enough," Megan said calmly, trying to reason with her brother. "I'll keep watch. Any trouble, we'll be back in the truck and on our way in seconds. You just keep the engine running."

Max didn't say another word. Julie was about to lose her cool with him when he eased up on the gas and pulled the vehicle to a stop on the side of the road.

"Be quick," he said gruffly.

Megan leaned over and kissed him on the cheek before getting out to scope out the surroundings.

As soon as she gave the all clear, Julie leaned over and opened the back door so that Maddie could get out. Reaching his arm in the backseat, he handed Julie a hunting knife.

"Just in case," he explained.

"Thank you."

Julie shuffled out of the truck, carefully so as not to jostle Sully and followed Megan and Maddie behind an abandoned car.

"Be as quick as you can, sweetheart," Julie said. "We'll keep a look out, okay?"

"Okay," Maddie mumbled, furtively looking around.

The poor girl had a right to be afraid, what she'd been through was more than anyone her age should have to deal with. Julie's blood boiled at the mere thought of it. She could only hope that her bastard of a stepfather got what he deserved.

While Julie and Megan waited for Maddie to finish, they thoroughly scanned their surroundings. Hearing movement from the woods, they swung around quickly to find two dead creatures limply ambling towards them. Mangled flesh hung from their bones; one had half of its face ripped off, the other, a missing arm.

Finally finished, Maddie walked around the side of the car and froze. Scooping her up, Julie quickly ran with her to the truck, Megan right behind them. As soon as Maddie and Julie were safely inside, Megan ran to the passenger side and had just managed to close her door when the creatures lurched against it.

"Go! Go! Go!" Megan yelled.

Max didn't need any further urging. Slamming his foot on the gas, he burned rubber and got them the hell out of there as quickly as possible. "Damn it, I knew it was a bad idea to stop."

"Don't start," Megan warned him.

"No more stops unless absolutely necessary. Understood?"

"She's a child and she had to go. Keep that in mind before you start acting like a jackass," Julie shot back.

"I love it when you get all fired up, Blondie." Sully joked, shifting himself into a different position.

Julie glared at him only to find herself completely disarmed by his gorgeous smile. She couldn't let on that he had any effect on her, so she just grunted, folded her arms around Maddie and closed her eyes.

SULLY

Sully chuckled and winced at the pain. *Damn, this wound still hurts like a bitch. Come to think of it, my whole body hurts*, he thought to himself, biting back the pain.

"Hey, Max, ease up on the ladies, will ya?" he said, trying to sit up straight.

"I'm only trying to make sure we all get to where we need to be—in one piece," Max shot back.

"I know you are. But she's a kid, so lay off."

Max caught his gaze in the mirror and nodded. Sully could tell the guy was stressed and was doing the best he could, but he wasn't about to let him off for scaring Maddie. Glancing over at the young girl and seeing her shaking in Julie's arms made him furious. He wanted to kill that bastard Connor with his bare hands. He'd taken more than just her innocence from her; he'd taken her hope—her spirit, the very essence of everything she could have become. Sully could see it in her eyes. They were lifeless and empty, yet at the same time full of pain and fear.

In normal circumstances, she may one day have been able to recover, to an extent, and be able to have as happy a life as she could. Now? Now she didn't have any fight left in her to be able to survive in the living nightmare that they were forced to deal with.

Sully watched as her shaking eased up while Julie stroked her hair. The woman was a Godsend. He didn't really believe in all that religious stuff, but he did believe in fate. He was meant to save her life, so that she could save Maddie. And if he could be a part of saving her, of bringing her back from whatever hell she'd retreated to in her mind, he would gladly do it. No child should have had to suffer through what she had in her short life.

"Behind us," Max said, breaking the silence. "There's a vehicle coming up fast."

Julie's eyes flew open as she and Sully both turned to look out the rear window. Struggling to see if he could identify the occupants, he could hear Megan in the front seat, loading and cocking her weapon—just in case.

As the vehicle drew close, Sully breathed a sigh of relief and grinned.

"It's Drew and the others," he confirmed.

30

Kate

Nathan turned to look at Kate, his eyes hooded. "What exactly do you need to tell us?" he asked warily.

Kate took a deep breath. She'd come this far, and she couldn't turn back now. They deserved to know.

"Kate, you don't have to say anything," Drew said.

"What the fuck is going on? Someone had damn well better tell me, and they better tell me right now," Nathan yelled, slamming his fist on the dashboard.

"Calm the fuck down, Nate," Drew warned.

"Why the hell should I? I know you've been hiding something, and I'm sick of it. We just lost a friend. I'm sick of the lies."

"Well, it's going to have to wait," Drew said with a smile. "Look ahead."

Up ahead, Kate could see Sully waving from the backseat of Max's truck and smiled with relief.

Nathan waved back briefly before turning to Kate, "You were saying."

Kate sighed. *There is no going back now.*

"I worked for the government on a special project. We were developing weapons that could be used in aerosol form if the need ever arose. These weapons had a virus in them. Unfortunately, the virus we developed was somehow released into the water supply. Consequently, the radiation from the virus also affected the weather patterns, setting off a string of storms, as well as infecting people who drank the tap water."

"You were a part of this?" Nathan asked, anger painting his face.

"I was part of a team who bio-engineered the virus. We didn't have time to test it. There was an imminent threat to our country from foreign entities and it was stolen before we could thoroughly test it."

"What happened to this virus?" Nathan queried.

"Once it hit the water, it mutated. We hadn't tested its reaction to other compounds yet. Basically, once ingested it affected people in different ways."

"How?" Nathan asked.

Kate took a breath. She could see anger, fear and confusion each play across his face. It was exactly how Drew had reacted; only Nathan was calmer, which scared her more.

"Some people became ill. Eventually, they died and their corpses reanimated. They became those things. Others weren't affected, but we later discovered that they didn't drink tap water as often as those who had turned did. And then, there were the special ones. The ones that developed special abilities."

"What sorts of abilities?" Drew asked.

"Some had super-human strength. Others—well, their features would change."

"Change? How?" Nathan asked.

"They would adopt wolf-like features, become strong, fast and would attack anyone endangering their loved ones. I changed when I watched my daughter die. I can't remember much, but I know I didn't get to her in time and that I killed all the corpses who had attacked her. Before running, I killed my baby girl. That's when Drew found me—I'd been on the run for a couple days."

Nathan was quiet. Too quiet. He just stared at her.

"I'm sorry, I know I'm responsible. I didn't have to say anything, but I thought you deserved to know the truth since I've witnessed both of you demonstrate some of the abilities. However, so far, they only seem to appear when you feel threatened, angry, or cornered. I don't think either of you have experienced the full potential of the abilities yet."

"Enough," Nathan said.

"I can help you both. I can show you, be there for you. We can be better prepared. The others need us to protect them."

"I said enough!" Nathan shouted, making everyone jump.

Drew swerved slightly and shot Nathan a dirty look. "Take a beat, Nate."

"She needs to stop talking. Now," he said through clenched teeth.

"Kate, leave him be for the time being," Drew said.

Doing as Drew had asked, Kate didn't say another word, she just sat back in her seat and glanced at Casey. The woman had been silent the whole time, however, the anger Kate saw in her expression scared her. She knew the best thing she could do right now was to shut up and let them process what she'd told them. *If I end up dead because of it, so be it. At least I told them the truth and someone else knows my dirty little secret*, she thought to herself, defeated. Pulling her legs up to her chest, Kate wrapped her arms around them and silently stared out the window.

NATHAN

Nathan was fuming. He was doing everything in his power not to embrace that anger and lash out at Kate. Turning away from her, he rolled down his window and inhaled deep breaths of the cold, damp air.

Drew knew better than to speak to him when he was like this. And for that, he was grateful. Nathan had too much love and respect for his friend to have him get caught in the crossfire between him and Kate. She was the one he was angry with. Or was he?

This entire time he'd wondered if the government had had something to do with all this shit. The hush-hush, the cover-ups, the unanswered questions—it all made sense now. However, it still riled him up knowing that Kate had been a part of it all.

Out of the blue, Casey began to cry, banging on the door. "Let me out. I'm going to be sick."

"Okay, okay, just hang on." Drew said. Flashing his lights at the other vehicle, he pulled to a stop. Before the car came to a complete halt, Casey flung open the door and ran into the woods.

"Casey—wait!" Nathan shouted. "Damn it, I'm going after her."

"Not alone, you're not," Drew said, grabbing his arm to stop him.

Nathan was grateful to see that the others had stopped and were making their way in their direction.

"Fine, I'll take Megan," Nathan said, pointing at the approaching woman.

"What's going on?" Megan asked, stopping at Nathan's open window.

"Casey said she was going to throw up. She just jumped out and ran into the woods."

"Damn, what the hell did she do that for? She could've just as easily thrown up on the road."

"I don't know. I need you to go with me to find her."

"That's probably not a good idea. We came across a few of those things a while back when we stopped for a bathroom break," Megan informed him.

"So, what, we just wait?"

"I'm not going in there unless I know what I'm walking into. In this weather, with minimal light and back-up, there's no way in hell I'm going anywhere," Megan replied adamantly.

"If something happens to her, it's on you," Nathan told Kate.

Getting out of the truck, he slammed the door behind him.

"What was that about?" Megan asked, following him to the edge of the woods.

"Nothing," Nathan grunted, staring into darkness beyond the treeline.

"I need to let the others know what's happening," Megan said. Patting him on the shoulder, she began to walk away when a scream stopped her in her tracks.

Before they could react, the dead came stumbling out of the woods.

"Get in! Quickly!" Drew yelled from the truck, flinging open the passenger door.

Megan had to half drag Nathan to the truck and shove him in. Before he could say anything, she slammed the door and made a run for the other vehicle.

DREW

"Roll up the windows," Drew ordered as he started the truck. Rolling forward slowly, he provided Megan with cover so she could make it back to the others. As soon as she was safely in the other truck, Drew sped up and took the lead, Max following close behind.

"Damn it! I should have gone after her," Nathan shouted.

"Nathan—there's nothing any of us could have done. It was her decision to run off somewhere we couldn't follow," Drew said.

Nathan turned toward him and Drew almost lost control of the vehicle.

"What the hell, bro?" Nathan growled.

"Your face."

Nathan looked in the rear-view mirror and jumped. Drew didn't blame him. His face now resembled a bad B-grade horror movie mask, only a hell of a lot more realistic and it couldn't just be removed.

Nathan looked at Drew again, his eyes glowing yellow. Slowly, his features began to change from wolf-like back to the Nathan he knew.

"This is what I was trying to tell you," Kate said excitedly. "Nathan, you're one of us. You're special. Those things don't stand a chance with us protecting the group. And we don't even know if any of the others have any abilities."

"Are you saying I'm going to turn into what he did? That you turn into that?" Drew asked, trying hard to process what he'd just seen and heard.

"No. You remember when the tree crashed into the building we were holed up in? You felt strong, didn't you? More so than usual?"

Drew thought back and realized she was right, he had felt more powerful than before. "So—I'm Superman now?"

"In a way. I wish I'd had more time to investigate and test other subjects."

"Subjects? Is that all we are to you? Experiments?" Nathan asked in anger.

"No, I didn't mean it like that. Old habits," Kate said calmly. "I just meant that I wish I knew more about this, about how it could have affected other people."

"Nathan, up ahead on the left. Are those survivors?" Drew interrupted, slowing down.

"Yeah, I think they are. Someone's flagging us down."

"Should we stop? Is it safe?" Kate asked worriedly.

"Drew, we have to take the chance. We've lost too many people, we need numbers," Nathan urged.

Drew knew he was right, he was still wary of the risk. That was until he was close enough to see who was flagging him down.

"I can't fucking believe it," Drew said, pulling the vehicle to the side of the road. "I found him."

31

Tyson

Motioning for Sam and Duke to join him, Tyson breathed a sigh of relief when the vehicles stopped. What he didn't expect was to hear a familiar voice.

"Ty? You're alive."

Tyson swung around to find Drew getting out of the first truck. "Drew! It's about fucking time," he joked.

Drew walked towards him and they hugged briefly. Tyson couldn't believe that his prayers had finally been answered; that his brother was alive and that they had somehow managed to find each other again. It was a miracle.

"Where the fuck have you been all this time?" Drew asked him, still clasping his shoulder.

"It's a long story, bro. We've kinda had a rough go of it and could do with a ride," Tyson replied, reigning in his emotions. By this time, Nathan had joined them, giving him a quick hug. Glancing around at everyone surrounding them, he couldn't see Sully or Shawn, just strangers. "Where's Shawn? Sully?"

"Sully's in the other truck. Someone finally shot his ass. He'll live, but he can barely move," Nathan explained.

"Shawn—he didn't make it," Drew said, pain etching his face.

"Damn—I'm sorry, Drew," Tyson replied, patting Drew on the shoulder in consolation.

"Who are your friends?" Nathan asked.

"This is Duke and Samantha...Sam. Duke, this is my brother, Drew, and our buddy, Nate."

"Can we cut the social niceties and get a fucking move on?" Max suddenly yelled out the window.

"Yeah, hold your horses, Max," Drew yelled back.

"We can squeeze one more in with us," Megan offered. "Maddie can sit on Julie's lap."

Drew nodded. "Good thinking. Ty, you're coming with us. We need to catch up."

"Yeah, okay. Sam? Duke?" Tyson asked.

"I'll go with them," Duke mumbled, walking towards Max's vehicle.

"Duke?" Tyson started after him only to have Sam stop him.

"Leave him be. He just needs some time," she suggested.

"Come on, let's go," Drew urged.

After everyone had huddled into their respective vehicles, they were on the road again within minutes.

32

Drew

Drew had so many questions racing through his mind. Ty looked like he'd been to hell and back, as did his companions. The last thing they needed was to be bombarded with a barrage of questions. At least not until they'd had some time to rest.

"Kate, this is my brother, Ty, and his friend, Samantha."

"It's Sam. Only Kelly called me Samantha," she corrected.

"Hi, Sam. Ty—it's nice to finally meet you. I've heard a lot about you," Kate said, shaking their hands.

"How did you hook up with my brother?" Tyson asked.

Nathan snorted, while Drew glared at him.

"Am I missing something?" Tyson asked.

"Kate and I ran into one another while I was out looking for you," Drew said.

"Drew saved my life. A couple times," Kate smiled.

"Likewise, sweetheart." Drew smiled back, winking at her in the mirror.

"In case you haven't figured it out, they're screwing each other," Nathan laughed.

"Nate! Not cool dude," Drew snapped.

"Sorry about our friend here, he was raised by wolves," Tyson apologized to Kate.

Drew looked at Nathan and caught Kate's eye in the mirror before bursting out laughing. Kate and Nathan soon followed suit.

"What the hell is so funny?" Tyson asked in confusion.

That only made the three of them laugh even harder.

"Sorry, bro, it's kinda an inside joke. We'll fill you in when everyone is together," Drew chuckled.

"Hey, you two hungry?" Kate asked their new companions.

"Not really, thank you though. I'm going to catch some shut eye," Sam said, turning to face the window.

"I could eat," Tyson said, accepting Kate's offer. "Thanks."

Drew exchanged a worried look with Nathan when Tyson wolfed down the food.

"When was the last time you ate anything, Ty?" Nathan asked worriedly.

"I can't remember. Must be days now," he said between mouthfuls.

"What happened to you when we got separated?" Drew asked.

Tyson stopped eating. "I made my way up into the mountains. Found a hunting lodge and broke into one of the cabins. I was going to hole up. Get some sleep and regroup. I didn't expect to run into Violet, but she was there. Almost stabbed me. She had no idea what was going on. Not a clue. We—we talked and then had to make a run for it when a horde of dead creatures swarmed the place. We barely escaped alive."

"Wait, Violet? Your ex-wife, Violet? Where is she? What happened?" Drew cut in, shocked.

"Yeah, Vi and I escaped. We were going to try to find you. We made a pit stop on the way and that's when I found Sam, Duke and Kelly. Not long after that we lost Violet. She'd been scratched by one of those things back at the cabin. We tried to help her. I prayed, but it wasn't enough. She begged me to kill her—to end her suffering. I didn't have a choice." Tyson broke down, his body wracked with sobs.

Drew was about to pull over when Kate reached for Tyson. Pulling him into her arms, she held him while he finally allowed his grief out.

"I loved her…I love her…I killed her…."

"Shhhh, it's okay," Kate cooed, gently stroking his hair.

Drew saw the pain in her eyes reflected in the mirror and he was grateful to her for offering his brother the comfort that he couldn't.

It wasn't long before Tyson was fast asleep in Kate's arms.

"Tyson saved us. We tried to be there for him with his wife, but he wouldn't let us," Sam piped up.

"How long ago did it happen?" Nathan asked softly.

"Must be a couple days now. Hard to tell, we haven't slept in a while," Sam replied.

"You mentioned Kelly. What happened to her?" Nathan pressed.

"She was my girlfriend. Duke's her father. We lost her just before y'all stopped to pick us up. She was probably still being eaten alive...." Sam trailed off.

"Damn—I'm sorry," Nathan said sincerely.

"We've all lost someone at some point or another in all this madness. Still isn't easy to get used to it," Sam said, closing her eyes.

NATHAN

Nathan turned to look at Kate. While he might not have liked what she'd had to say, the way people were dropping off around them, it was nice to have someone around who knew what the fuck was going on.

"Kate," he said, "I'm sorry for how I reacted earlier."

Kate smiled at him. It was a sad, sweet smile. "I know. It's okay. It was a lot to take in."

"Doesn't excuse how I behaved."

"Forget it. Maybe now we can work together to try and make sense of this whole thing," she suggested.

"Thank you," Nathan said, reaching out to squeeze her hand.

"I'll just kick your ass next time you step outta line," she joked, winking at him.

"I don't doubt that you could, little lady," Nathan laughed softly.

"Now that you guys have made friends again, can we focus on where we're going and how we're going to get there," Drew said.

"Sir, yes, Sir," Nathan and Kate both said in unison, chuckling at the look on Drew's face.

"Great, I'm stuck with two smartasses," he groaned.

Nathan playfully punched him in the shoulder. "We just can't win, Kate. He's upset when we're fighting and now he's upset that we've made up."

"Some guys are so hard to please," Kate said playfully.

"Trust me, sweetheart, you don't have any problems pleasing me," Drew drawled suggestively.

"I did not need to hear that," Nathan said, groaning and covering his ears.

Kate reached over and slapped them both upside the head.

"I have to hand it to you, Drew, she is a feisty one," Nathan laughed.

"Damn!" Drew said, putting a halt to the joking.

Looking ahead Nathan quickly spotted the issue. A long-haul truck had tipped over and was blocking the roadway in front of them. There were a few cars littered on either side, but nowhere for them to maneuver.

Drew had no choice but to pull over.

"We're gonna have to move those cars and pray that the road ahead is clear," Nathan said.

"Yeah—we need to be smart about this. If anything goes wrong, we need people behind the wheels, ready to go," Drew added. "Let's talk to Max and see what he suggests."

"I'll go have a chat with him. Stay here," Nathan said, hopping out of the truck and walking over to Max.

"What's up?" Max asked, rolling down his window. "We aren't going to get far if we keep stopping."

"I know, but this time we don't have a choice. Road's blocked."

"Shit. Got a plan?"

"A few of us need to move the cars on either side of the truck while someone stays behind in each vehicle in case we need to make a break for it."

"Okay, let's get to it. Duke, you okay to hop behind the wheel while Megan and I go help?"

"Yeah, of course," Duke replied.

Nathan and the siblings made their way over to Drew.

"Sam's going to man the wheel while the rest of us move those cars," Drew said.

"Right. Well, let's get to it," Max said.

Between the six of them, they managed to successfully clear a path around the overturned truck in no time. Just as they were moving the last car they began to make out the moaning above the wind and rain.

Nathan swung around quickly, only to find a horde of the undead between them and their trucks.

K ate swung into action. Pulling her knife, she stepped forward.

"There are too many of them," Megan yelled.

"Nathan? You ready?" Kate asked, ignoring her.

"Ready to do what?" he asked in confusion.

"Take these bastards out?"

"How?"

"Change. Get riled up. You'll know what to do," Kate said.

"What about me?" Drew asked, grabbing her arm.

"Use your strength. Use your anger," she told him. "We can do this."

Thinking about her daughter, Kate pictured her death and how it had felt to lose her in that moment. It did the trick. Feeling her face transform, she felt herself become stronger. Reeling with anger, she attacked.

One after the other, she ripped and clawed, stabbed and slashed her way through the masses of slobbering, mindless freaks snapping at her.

From the corner of her eye she could see Nathan and Drew doing the same. They were formidable; a team working in unison to eradicate the threat to the people they cared about.

Together the three of them provided enough of a distraction so that the others could finish moving the last vehicle out of the way.

Sweeping the legs out from under the last one, Kate pounced on it, pinning it down so that Nathan could kill it. Looking up at him, she smiled through fanged teeth. As Nathan helped her up, she looked around at the mangled corpses. The threat had been eliminated just as she'd thought it would be. While the others began running back to the trucks, she hung back with Nathan.

"You know you want to," she said, grinning.

With a sly smile, Nathan threw back his head and let out a celebratory howl.

Not one to be left out of the fun, Kate soon joined in the celebration.

"You guys coming or are you just gonna stand here howling?" Drew asked.

Kate's howl began to fade as she felt her features return to normal. "We're done. Let's go."

As they made their way back to the vehicle Nathan and joined in a high-five.

"What the hell was that?" Tyson asked once they were safely back inside the truck and on the road again.

Placing his arm around Kate, Drew nodded. Smiling, she began explaining her story to Tyson and Sam. Once she'd explained everything, she took Drew's hand and waited for the onslaught of verbal abuse and accusations. But they never came.

"So, everyone can do what you guys just did?" Tyson asked.

"I don't know. I wish I did, but in all honesty, I don't know what the long term affects are, or why it affects people in different ways. All I managed to discover before it was too late was that it's down to genetics."

"So, this thing may eventually kill us?" Nathan asked.

"Honestly? I don't have a clue. And until I have access to a lab and equipment so I can run some tests—I won't know."

"Okay, so we find the stuff you need and take it with us," Nathan suggested.

"They aren't just things we'd find at the local drug store, Nate."

"So, where would we find the stuff you need?" he asked.

"A hospital, a college or high school science lab…but all of those places would more than likely have loads of the dead walking around them," Kate said. "Besides, to do those kind of tests, I'd need machines, computers, chemicals and secure testing facilities. It's just not feasible with things the way they are."

"Kate's right. It's a nice idea, and one to look at once we're settled somewhere, but right now that is our main priority—to find somewhere we can feel safe and try to make a life, away from all of this," Drew said.

"So where are we headed?" Sam asked.

"New Orleans," Nathan confirmed.

DREW

Pulling Kate closer, Drew kissed her on the forehead, smiling when she leaned into him, laying her head on his chest.

This woman had driven him crazy ever since he'd picked her up on the side of the road, but it was a good kind of crazy. She wasn't his usual type, however, that was probably a good thing. Kate sighed, snuggling closer while sleepily mumbling his name.

"You like her," Tyson whispered softly.

Looking at his brother, Drew could see the sadness in his eyes. He looked defeated, and it worried him.

"Yeah, I like her," Drew confirmed. "I'm sorry about Violet."

"So am I. Running into her was like fate or something, man. We talked about Gracie—we reconnected. I felt something for her, always have and always will. I knew it was too good to be true. Second chance my ass! There's no such thing."

"Ty, you had those moments. At least she didn't die alone," Drew said softly.

"When I...we...lost Gracie, I thought my life was over. I pushed Violet away. It was my fault she left. I lost my child and my wife in that accident. And then Ellie…" Tyson choked up, taking a moment to regain his composure. "When I found Vi again, it was like God had granted me another chance. I felt alive again. I allowed myself to love, to hope, to live. Then all of that was ripped from me again. In that moment that I pulled the trigger, I may as well have killed myself. I almost did, but Duke talked me down and convinced me to go on. I even gave up on ever finding you. Honestly, I figured you were dead," Tyson confessed.

Drew's heart broke for his brother. Everything he'd been through, all the suffering, the loss. He wished he could do something, anything, to take away his pain.

"We did find each other though, Ty. We're together now and I've got your back. And I know damn well you've got mine."

"Thanks, bro."

Looking at Sam, Drew spoke. "I'm gonna catch some shut eye and then I'll take over driving."

"Sure, I'm good for now," she replied.

NATHAN

Nathan was lost in his thoughts, staring out the window, trying to make sense of everything.

"You know these guys long?" Sam asked him.

"Yeah, most of my life. We went to school together and have been friends ever since," Nathan replied.

"I had a couple buddies like that in the Army. No idea where they are now—or if they're even alive."

"Yeah, things sure are different now," Nathan laughed dryly.

"That's one way of putting it."

"Why New Orleans?" she asked, glancing sideways at him.

"It's the only place I could think of that offered the safest solution possible. I know the risk getting there, but once we're there, we might actually stand a chance."

"And just how are we supposed to get to this island?"

"We borrow a boat."

"Easier said than done. How do you know others haven't had the same idea? Or if there are even any boats left?"

"I don't. I just have to believe that things will work out," Nathan said.

They drove in silence for a while, Sam occasionally dodging creepers that were wandering into the road. They were making good time, no more obstacles, when the fuel light suddenly flashed on the console.

"Fuck," Sam muttered.

"What's up?" Nathan asked, sitting up straight.

"Fuel's low. You guys have any spare?"

"One container. We're gonna need to scrounge some more eventually."

"There are vehicles up ahead. Maybe we can siphon some," Sam suggested.

"Okay, pull up just past those cars. We don't want to get boxed in if we get attacked."

"Sure thing. Your buddy Max isn't going to be too happy about us stopping," Sam sighed.

"Let me handle him." Nathan said.

Sam pulled up just beyond the cluster of abandoned vehicles and put the truck into park.

The other vehicle screeched to a halt beside them and Max jumped out, angrily slamming the car door behind him.

"What the fuck is wrong now?" Max yelled.

"Keep it down! You wanna wake the dead?" Nathan growled, grabbing his arm.

"Get the fuck off me."

"I will—when you calm the fuck down."

"Fine. What seems to be the problem now?" Max asked sarcastically.

Nathan stared at him in disgust. "We need to refuel. Our light flashed on. Figured this was the safest place to stop."

"Our fuel is getting low too, Max. They made a good call," Megan said, coming around to calm her brother down.

"Fine. Just make it quick."

"What is your problem, buddy?"

"You are! This whole plan is stupid. We've been shot at, attacked by the dead, lost people, some of you are fucking freaks of nature and no one seems to be in a rush to find safety. How long do you think we're gonna last out here in the open?"

"Hey, we're doing the best we can. We've all lost people. We can only go as fast and as far as we can without obstacles. We can't control those. As for us *freaks*, you think that's our fault? We never asked for any of this. This is all the governments fault. Ask Kate, she'll tell you," Nathan shouted, losing his cool.

"What the fuck does she have to do with it?" Max asked, his fists clenched in anger.

"I was part of a scientific team that engineered the virus that caused all of this. If you'll just let me explain—" Kate didn't have a chance to finish her sentence before Max reached for her and slammed her up against the side of their truck. Kate cried out in pain at the force of the impact.

Max didn't know what hit him. One minute he had his hands on Kate, the next he was launched away from her and thrown onto the hood of one of the abandoned cars.

"You touch her again and I will kill you," Drew threatened, lifting Kate into his arms and placing her gently in the back of their vehicle.

"Okay, everyone take a beat. We need to work together, not attack each other," Megan said, stepping between her brother and the others.

"Let's just get the fuel and get outta here. We can find somewhere to hole up and have a chat," Nathan said, grabbing a hose and container from the back of the truck.

"Take the other container and start siphoning from those cars while I fill up with this one."

"Got it," Tyson said.

Sam and Duke joined Tyson to help keep watch while Megan took her brother aside and gave him a talking to.

Nathan watched them whispering and gesturing furiously. "That guy could be a loose cannon, Drew."

"Yeah. We're gonna need to keep an eye on him."

"Is she okay?" Nathan asked.

"I think so. She's gonna be bruised," Drew scowled. "I know she had a hand in this, Nate, but it wasn't her fault. It's not right for her to feel as though it is. She lost her daughter for God's sake."

"Look, she's the only one who knows what the fuck is going on. You expect me to just forget about everything she said? The others deserve to know the truth."

"And they will, but not right now. We can't let our emotions and tempers get the best of us in an environment we can't control."

"Agreed. We do need to think about somewhere to hole up so we can all get some proper rest."

"Hey, I might know somewhere," Julie piped up from inside the car. "There's a library, a couple towns over. It's secure and on the way to New Orleans."

"Okay, you show Nate on the map and we'll pack up," Drew said.

Half an hour later both trucks were fuelled up with extra gas in the containers. Driving off in the direction of the library, they prayed they would get the chance to rest and recharge.

34

Max

"There it is," Julie said, pointing to a large brownstone building.

"Thank God," Sully sighed. "I could use a break from being jostled about on the road."

They had been travelling for hours, the streets were getting dark and the shadows seemed to be multiplying. Max had remained silent the entire journey, not even acknowledging his sister. He could tell Megan was fed up with his attitude based upon the dirty looks she kept throwing at him. Still, he remained silent. The stress and uncertainty of the last few weeks were finally catching up to him.

Max could sense he was at breaking point and that scared him. Truth be told, he carried immense guilt over losing the last of their family, he didn't want to have to worry about the possibility of losing his sister due to other people's stupidity.

"Max, you stay here with Julie, Sully and Maddie. I'll go with the others to make sure it's safe inside," Megan said.

"Like hell! You stay here and babysit, I'm going in," Max argued as they parked near the steps of the library.

"What, so you can get your ass killed for being a jerk?"

"Look, you may be my sister, but I'm not about to take orders from you. Never have. Never will."

"Carry on the way you are and you won't have to worry about me bossing you around ever again."

"What is that supposed to mean?"

"Just fuck off," Megan snapped, checking her gun.

Max and Duke stepped out of the car to join the others. Kate had volunteered to stay and help Megan. Of to the side, stewing in anger, Max watched as Drew pulled Kate into his arms and kissed her soundly before leading the others up the library steps.

The building was grand, featuring ornate railings, solid oak doors with elaborate brass rings and intricate etchings on each one.

"One at a time, stay in sight of one another. Ready?" Drew instructed. When the others nodded in agreement, he opened one of the doors slowly, flashlight in one hand, gun in the other.

One by one they entered the darkened building, sweeping the beams of their flashlights as they advanced into the room.

Drew motioned for each of them to search the aisles and they progressed. As they advanced into the room they were able to make out faint noises towards the rear of the building. Drew moved forward but Max quickly jumped ahead of him, pushing forward, oblivious to anyone or anything else. If he was on a mission to get himself killed then he was heading in the right direction.

"Max," Drew hissed.

Max simply waved him off and kept going. He wasn't about to take orders from anyone, not when his sister's life was at stake. Besides, he knew how to handle himself. He'd gotten them this far and they were still alive. So cocksure was Max that he didn't even notice the creeper until it was on him.

In the scuffle he watched as Drew and Tyson ran towards him only for more creatures to appear, blocking their path. Between the five of them, they made quick work in killing the undead.

While the others were attempting to clear a path to Max, he continued to struggle with the creature, losing his gun in the process. Before he could retrieve his weapon and put an end to the flesh-eating beast he felt searing pain, as his stomach was ripped open. His final thought before death itself latched onto his throat and life left him was of Megan.

Drew had just managed to get close enough to fire a headshot at the dead *thing* attacking Max. He watched as the force of the bullet connected with its oozing flesh, propelling it away from Max's prone body.

"Max? You okay?" Drew asked, falling to his knees at the man's side. He shone his flashlight at the man when he didn't answer and had to look away. Max's throat was a bloody mess and his stomach was ripped open, his innards spilling out. There was blood everywhere.

Nathan checked for a pulse but he was already gone. Saying a quick prayer, Drew could only watch in silence as Nathan slid a knife into Max's brain, ensuring he would not return to become one of those *things*.

"Come on, we need to move these bodies so the others can come in. Drew, go get Megan so she can say goodbye before we deal with his body," Nathan said stoically.

While the others moved the dead and cleaned up as much as possible, Drew brought Megan in to say goodbye to her brother. He prepared her as best as he could but he knew nothing he said would ease the horror she would experience at the sight of her brother's mutilated body.

"Who made sure he wouldn't come back?" she asked, her voice emotionless.

"I did. I'm sorry—" Nathan said, stepping closer.

Megan turned and slapped him. Stepping forward, Drew attempted to intervene but Nathan halted him. Megan looked at them, shocked, tears streaming down her face. Collapsing into Nathan's arms, she began sobbing uncontrollably.

Taking the sobbing woman into his arms, Nathan quickly moved her away so that Drew and Tyson could move Max's body. He continued to hold her while they brought the supplies in, securing the windows and the entrance.

KATE

Making Sully as comfortable as possible, Kate examined and redressed his wound while Julie watched from a distance.

"It looks good. Stitches are holding and there doesn't appear to be any infection," Kate confirmed, applying a fresh dressing.

"Thank God for that. How long before I can move without it hurting like a bitch?" Sully groaned.

"You should be okay by the time we make it to New Orleans," Kate smiled.

"Great! Thanks, doc," Sully said.

Once Kate was finished, Julie sat down next to Sully, Maddie following suit. Kate watched as the young girl huddled close to Julie. It broke her heart to see such fear in the girl's eyes.

"Maddie, do you need anything?"

"No, thank you," she whispered.

"Okay, I'll be over there if you do," Kate said, exchanging a look with Julie.

"I've got it from here," Julie reassured Kate, giving Maddie a squeeze.

Kate nodded and walked over to join Drew and Nathan, who had finally managed to calm Megan enough that she was resting in the corner.

"Everyone's pretty low right now," Kate said, moving into Drew's arms. "Maybe you should say something."

"Yeah, I need a minute to think, sweetheart," Drew said, leaning down to give her kiss.

She smiled. "Okay. I'll sort some food out for everyone. Give me a hand, Nate?"

Together they managed to scrounge together a decent meal for everyone, the room silent other than the sounds of scraping tins. Even with their hunger temporarily sated, there was silence fraught with hunger. Not a physical hunger; an emotional and spiritual one that had not been sated for far too long. They were starving from a lack of hope and faith.

DREW

Drew stood beside the boarded-up window and watched as their small group gathered in a circle on the library floor, one solitary lantern providing a dim glow of light, which as much as they could chance. He could sense their weariness and could see the despair etched upon their faces.

"I know it's been a long journey, and it's far from over, but we're still here."

Drew took a step towards them, futilely wiping his dirty hands on his even dirtier clothes.

"We've lost people, every one of us has lost somebody along the way, but we've also found people; new friends and family. This ain't gonna be it for us. Once we get to New Orleans, get a handle on a boat, and find that island, we're gonna be able to live again. Really live. We just can't give up. We gotta keep going. The people we've lost would want us to survive, to live. We gotta do it for them as much as we've gotta do it for us."

In one corner of the group Maddie began to cry. The little girl huddled even closer to Julie while Sully stroked her hair. Drew's heart ached for the girl. The things she'd witnessed left him cold.

"The things we've seen, the things we've had to do to get here——no one should ever have to go through what we have. But we have. And we're still here. We've survived. We are survivors. That's what will get us to that island, alive and together. Each and every person here has a reason to get there, a reason to survive and a reason to fight. Don't forget it. Even when we come up against those creatures out there, even when they come at us, when the living turn against us, when we can't hear ourselves think over the noise of these fucking storms—even then, we can't give up. Giving up means you're as good as dead. And if you're as good as dead, then you ain't one of us. So now is the time. Either you're a survivor and you want to live, to fight, to be one of us; or you're as good as dead and you're dead weight. If you're dead weight, you can't drag the rest of us down. You gotta cut and run, or stay and hide, whichever suits you best. Decide. Decide now because tomorrow morning we're hitting the road again and this time we ain't stopping till we get to the coast."

Drew saw shock on some of their faces. The only people who weren't shocked were the ones he knew would make it. What surprised him was that his brother wasn't one of them. The sound of rain battering the windows almost drowned out the sound of the thunder rumbling ominously in the distance. Unfortunately, it didn't quiet Drew's mind though. There wasn't anything that could do that.

"We've all come a long way since the shit hit the fan. Some of you I didn't reckon would make it this far, but you have. And that is why I think you can make it the rest of the way. Don't give up now. I know you've lost everything, or you think you have. But you haven't. You've still got us. All of us. We're family now. We're bound together by something stronger than blood; we're bound by desire, drive and fight. The need to be together, to stay together. We ain't dead. We're alive. Our hearts are beating, and while there is still blood pumping through our veins and the tiniest of thoughts running through our tired minds—we have a chance. We can end this. We just have to stick together and keep on keeping on."

Drew stared at Tyson, willing him to hear his words. He needed his brother to fight. He needed him to want to live.

"Y'all with me?"

One by one everyone nodded. Looking to his brother, Tyson looked at him and Drew could see that he was struggling to decide. "Ty?"

"Yeah, I'm with you," Tyson replied, smiling sadly.

"Good, now get some rest while you can. I'll take first shift," Drew said, walking back toward the window.

"Hey, you sure you want me around?" Tyson asked, following behind him.

Drew turned to look at his brother. He didn't say anything; he simply pulled him into his arms and held him.

Tyson patted Drew on the back and stepped back. "Thank you," he said sincerely.

Drew watched as he made his way back over to Sam and Duke to settle down and get some rest, along with everyone else.

If this is the way life has to be from now on, I will do everything in my power to keep the rest of them together and to not lose anyone else. I will get them to that island, and to safety, if it is the last thing I do.

36

Drew

The water was turbulent as wind and rain battered their speedboat. The last three days had taken a toll on them. By the time they had made it to New Orleans and managed to find a working boat, they had been attacked numerous times by the undead.

Drew gazed back at the burning dock. They had been ambushed as they were fuelling up the boat, and Sam had managed to sneak around to create a diversion so that the others could get to safety. Tyson tried to rescue her, but she had screamed at him to go. Drew and Nathan had to forcibly drag him onto the boat. They were still near the dock when they heard the gunshot, followed by the full force of an explosion.

In the back of the boat, Drew could see Tyson sitting, huddled and silent. He could clearly see death reflected in his brother's eyes, and that scared him. Drew couldn't force his brother to want to live, but he sure as hell wasn't about to let him die without a fight.

All around him, his friends were sitting, shaking, holding on for dear life as the boat sped over choppy waters.

"How far to this island?" Drew shouted, leaning towards Nathan.

Nathan was struggling to maintain control of the wheel so Drew grabbed hold to give him a hand.

"An hour, maybe less," Nathan yelled back.

There was no point attempting further conversation with the wind sweeping their words away.

Turning back to the crowd of people, Drew watched as Kate and Julie both held onto Maddie, trying to shield her from the stinging rain. Across from them, Tyson wasn't even bothering to shield himself from the battering winds and rain. His face was red and his hands were blue. Catching Duke's eyes, Drew exchanged a worried look with him. It was obvious the man considered Tyson to be the son he never had. Moving closer to Tyson, Duke put his arm around him and didn't let go, even when Tyson struggled. Nodding, Drew smiled at Duke, grateful that he was there to comfort his mule-headed brother.

NATHAN

The next hour was quite possibly the longest and the most physically testing hour of their lives. A majority of them were numb, being attacked at all angles from the elements.

When they finally saw land, Nathan wanted to cry in relief. He was equally pleased that the rain was beginning to ease up the closer they got to the island.

Slowing the boat, Nathan began scouring the area looking for a dock. His heart sank when he found it. There were already three other boats docked there.

"We could have a problem," Nathan shouted.

"We'll handle it," Drew replied.

Docking the boat, they gathered their meager belongings and exited. Once on dry land, everyone ensured their weapons were loaded and at the ready.

"We stick together and move quickly. If we come across anyone still alive, let me do the talking," Drew said, securing the straps on his backpack, and drawing his gun.

Making their way up a sandy beach towards what looked to be a path, they following it through woods to a clearing on a small hill.

Once atop the hill, everyone stopped, mouths agape as they surveyed what lay below them in a valley. Lush green hills, an orchard and what appeared to be vegetable gardens, along with houses, at least forty of them, with a park in the middle lie before their eyes.

"Fucking hell! I didn't expect this," Nathan breathed, not believing what he was seeing.

"I can't see if there are people down there, so we go steady. We don't want to walk into anything we can't handle." Drew said.

Slowly they trekked down the hill towards the homes on constant alert for any movement. Making their way past the gardens and orchards, they continued into the center of the town.

"Stop right there," a man shouted as he stepped out from behind a tree.

"We don't want any trouble," Drew said, putting his hands up. "We're just looking for shelter."

"You sure are packing a lot of fire power for people not looking for any trouble," the man replied, doubtfully.

"Sorry, we weren't sure what to expect with everything going on back on the mainland," Drew explained.

"Is it bad?" the man asked, stepping forward.

"Yeah, it is," Drew replied honestly.

"Okay, how about we put the guns away and then continue this little chat indoors," the man suggested.

Motioning for everyone to holster their weapons, Drew and the others followed the man into the building. Inside were other people, all seated at tables, immersed in their meals.

"You guys hungry?"

"Starving," Julie said. "We ran out of food last night."

"I'll get you sorted," he said, motioning to a young woman. "I'm Adam, by the way."

Shaking his hand, Nathan quickly introduced the group. Stepping to the side for a moment, Adam had a quick word with the woman who quickly hurried off towards what he assumed was the kitchen. Motioning to one of the tables, everyone sat, grateful for the gesture.

"How long have y'all been here?" Nathan asked.

"Almost since the beginning. I worked for the architectural company that designed this place. It was meant to be a secure environmental experiment facility. People would be chosen to move here for a five-year period. No technology, no communications, just a tight-knit community with the basics. When the world went to shit, I gathered my family and friends, a few people we met on the way, and we ferried everyone over. Thankfully, the vegetable gardens and orchards had already been planted weeks before and the larder stocked. We even have cows, chickens, pigs and sheep."

A few moments later a couple of women arrived with plates laden with hot, freshly cooked food. The minute Nathan got a whiff of the food, his stomach growled.

"Go on, tuck in. I'll get you all some drinks. Soda okay?" Adam asked, standing up.

Everyone nodded, mouths full. Even Maddie, who hadn't eaten in days, was ravenously attacking the food, which was a relief to everyone to see her eating at last.

"What do you make of all of this?" Nathan asked softly.

"Not sure yet. I can't get a read on the guy," Drew answered.

It wasn't long before Adam returned with a case of soda, quickly handing them out. Setting the rest on a nearby table, he sat down to join them once again..

"So, I need to ask you guys a few questions. Just to make sure you're on the up and up. We haven't had anyone new show up in weeks. Not many people know about this place."

"Sure, what do ya need to know?" Nathan asked.

"How long have you all been together?"

Drew glanced around the table. Nathan nodded, catching Drew's eyes, encouraging him to take the lead. "Since the beginning. Tyson is my brother. Sully and Nate are our best friends, Kate is my girl, Julie is Sully's, Megan is Nate's. Duke is an old friend and Maddie is a relative of Julie's. We're all family one way or another. We've lost other friends and family along the way."

"Have any of you taken a human life?"

"Only in self-defense, and even then, not many. Only when there was no other option," Drew confirmed.

"Okay, and how did you know about this island?"

"I was a fireman. I had a contact higher up who knew all about it. Wanted to recommend me for the experiment. I forgot about it till a week or so ago, didn't think anyone else would be here, or if it would be overrun," Nathan cut in.

"Would you be willing to give up your guns in order to stay here?"

"As long as we can keep our hunting knives, yes."

"Fair enough. We all keep knives on us, just in case. It's the guns we shy away from."

Once everyone had finished their meals they each handed their guns and ammo, Tyson more reluctantly than the others.

"Great, if you ever want to leave or go to the mainland, you'll get them back."

"So, what now?" Drew asked.

"You all look like you could do with some decent sleep. Why don't I take you to the houses? We have spares, as long as some of you don't mind sharing. Most of the houses are two bedrooms, but we have some with three. Figure you'd want to stick together till you get to know us."

"That would be appreciated. Thank you, Adam," Nathan said gratefully.

They all stood, following Adam outside as he guided them towards the island's housing. Thankfully, it wasn't a long walk.

Stopping in front of a beautiful house with a wrap-around porch, Adam spoke. "This is one of our three-bedroom houses. There is another one right next door with an adjoining backyard. The doors are open. Make yourselves at home. We can all meet up tomorrow at lunch to introduce you to everyone else."

"Thanks, man. We appreciate it," Drew said, shaking his hand.

Turning to the group, Nathan smiled. "Right, who is going where?"

"Why don't Kate and I, as well as Julie, Sully, Tyson and Maddie take this one? Nate, you can go with Duke and Megan in the other house," Drew quickly suggested.

"Everyone okay with that?" Nate asked, relieved that no one objected to the living arrangements.

"Nate, could you give us a hand before you go?" Drew asked him.

"Sure," he replied before they all went their separate ways.

Nathan was the first to enter. It had been a long time since he'd been in a house that was in one piece; not storm ravaged or looted to high hell with blood and decomposing flesh stinking up the place.

Instead, he stepped into a pristinely decorated room that smelled of fresh flowers. As they toured the house, they found each room was impeccably decorated.

"Let's get Sully settled in bed before he passes out," Julie finally said, struggling to support the injured man.

"Nate, give me a hand," Drew asked, slipping his arm under Sully's.

Together, they helped Sully into bed and allowed Kate to check his wound and dressings before leaving him to sleep.

It was agreed that Julie and Maddie would take the room next door, leaving Kate and Drew with the master bedroom.

"Where am I supposed to sleep?" Ty asked.

"Figured you could bunk down with Sully," Drew suggested.

"No way. To be honest, I'd rather just go next door, as long as you're okay with me sleeping on the couch," Tyson suggested, looking directly at Nathan.

"Ty—I thought maybe we could talk later," Drew finally said.

"About what? I'm done talking. I did my part. I got y'all here...I'm done," Tyson said before walking away.

"Ty—" Drew called after him.

The door slamming was his only reply.

"Give him some time," Kate said softly, wrapping her arm around Drew's waist. Draping his arm over her shoulder, he sighed.

"I'll keep an eye on him, bro," Nathan promised, giving Drew a quick pat on the back before following Tyson.

It would be a long road back for Tyson, especially considering everything he'd been through. Unfortunately, it was quite obvious that it was a road he wasn't ready to go down yet. *Maybe Kate is right and he just needs some time to get his head and heart right. I have to trust that Tyson will come to me when he is ready.*

Right now, Nathan just wanted to get back to Megan and make sure that she was okay. Over the last few days they had become very close, but the death of her brother had a left a void that he was desperately trying to fill with all the love and support he could give her. Regardless of what the future held for them, all he knew for sure was that he wanted Megan to be a part of his.

ONE YEAR LATER

Kate rolled over and snuggled against Drew. It was early and they still had some time before the house would be awake. Tracing his tight abdomen lazily with her fingers, she lightly kissing his chest.

"Are you trying to kill me, woman?" Drew growled. Rolling over on top of her, he took her by surprise.

Kate squealed, smiling as he settled himself above her.

"Mr. Hawkins, I know that's not your gun, so you must be happy to see me," she giggled.

"Indeed, I am, Mrs. Hawkins," he smiled, pressing his hard cock against her thigh.

Even after a year together, their sex life was still just as intense as ever. Just one of her husband's smoldering looks was enough to turn her on.

Linking her hands behind his head, she pulled him in for a kiss.

Suddenly, the sound of crying broke through their passionate haze. Groaning, Drew lifted himself off of her.

"Impeccable timing as usual," Kate laughed, getting out of bed and slipping on her robe.

"Hurry back, gorgeous."

"I will," Kate winked. Stepping out into the hallway, she swung open the door to the room next door.

"What's the matter, sweetpea?" she asked softly, reaching into the crib and picking up her two-month-old daughter. Once in her arms, Kate snuggled against Ellie, who immediately stopped crying.

"You just needed a cuddle with your mama, didn't you, honey?" Kate said, her heart filled with overwhelming love for the soft bundle in her arms. Settling Ellie into her arms, she quietly made her way back to bed and gently handed her to Drew.

She is definitely going to be daddy's little girl, she thought to herself as she watched her husband and daughters interaction. She'd had him wrapped around her little finger from the very first moment he'd seen her. They decided to name her after Drew and Tyson's baby sister, in her honor.

Life had certainly changed for all of them after they'd arrived on Genesis Island. It had taken a while for them to get used to being in a civilized environment again, and around other people. After a few months, it began to feel more like home. Still, they were all silently waiting for the other shoe to drop—for something to go wrong.

A few months after their arrival, Kate and Drew were married by the island minister. Sully and Julie followed suit not long after. Julie and Sully had adopted Maddie as their own, and with a lot of help and patience, she slowly came to trust and love Sully. He had become the father figure she should have had from the beginning. Now, Julie was pregnant, and Maddie was looking forward to having a younger sibling to look after.

Nathan and Megan were on again, off again. Kate knew that deep down a part of Megan would always blame Nathan for her brother's death, even if she knew otherwise. Sadly, Duke passed away in his sleep a month after they'd arrived. The strain of losing his wife, his daughter and then Sam, had been too much for him to bear and his heart gave out.

Tyson had a hard time with things. He fought with Drew constantly, started drinking heavily and causing disturbances. He came extremely close to being kicked off the island. When Ellie was born, he took one look at her and he broke down. Tyson and Drew made amends soon after and he moved in with them.

Tyson wanted to be there for his niece, to watch her grow up and protect her. Kate secretly wondered if his resolve to make certain nothing bad ever happened to Ellie was due to the loss of his daughter and wife. His way of making sure history didn't repeat itself. Still, it warmed her heart watching him with Ellie. In spite of everything, Tyson was a good man, and Kate knew that if anything ever happened to her or to Drew, she'd be content leaving her daughter with Tyson to raise.

"What time are we meeting the others?" Kate asked, curling up in bed with her family.

"Couple of hours," Drew replied, glancing at his watch. Settling Ellie between them, he reached over to stroke Kate's cheek. "I love you."

"I love you too, handsome. You and Ellie both. So much," Kate replied, her eyes tearing up.

Drew smiled and leaned in for a kiss. As though she planned it perfectly, Ellie gurgled, and they broke apart laughing. Scooping their daughter up into his arms, Drew showered her with kisses.

Kate loved watching Drew with their little girl. He was so good with her. Standing up, she made her way over to the window. In the street below, people were milling about, headed to the mess hall for breakfast before their day began.

"We should get ready," Kate said. "Could you change Ellie while I get dressed. Then I'll feed her."

"Sure thing, babe."

An hour later, all three of them were dressed and headed out the door. Heading towards the beach, Drew still couldn't believe how different life had become over the last year. He'd become a husband, a father, re-established a relationship with his brother, and watched his friends fall in love. Life was good.

Like Kate, he was worried about the other shoe dropping, which is why they kept a secret stash of weapons and supplies buried down by the docks. They also ensured that they never left their homes without their backpacks filled with clothes, water, flashlights and their knives.

Perhaps they were paranoid, but there was always a chance, however slim, that things could take a turn for the worse. While it was a small chance, they all preferred to be prepared, rather than to be caught unaware.

"Here they are," Sully cheered as they approached.

They had a picnic blanket set up and Julie and Maddie were each sitting on a corner. A short distance away, Tyson, Nathan, and Megan were kicking a ball around.

Jogging over, Tyson quickly scooped his niece from Kate's arms. "How's my baby girl?"

"She's good, Ty," Kate laughed, sitting down next to Julie.

"I'm so glad the weather's been good the last few months," Julie said, leaning back to enjoy the sun.

"You okay, Maddie?" Kate asked.

"I'm good, Aunt Kate," Maddie smiled.

"Ooph," Julie grunted. "Sully, your child is kicking up a storm today."

"That's my boy," Sully said, leaning down to rub his wife's belly.

"I still think it's a girl," Julie muttered, pulling a face.

Kate laughed. It would serve Sully right if they did have a girl. He would be outnumbered and completely wrapped around each female's finger in one way or another.

"Hey, Ty—how are things with Lily?" Drew asked.

"Things are good. We're taking it slow," Tyson said, staring up the beach. "Speak of the devil, here she comes."

DREW

In the distance Drew could see Lily running towards them, fast. One look behind her and Drew's blood ran cold.

"Everyone up. Now! Get to the supplies and the boat," Drew ordered. "Ty, Nate, Meg you stay and help."

Tyson quickly handed Ellie to Kate while Sully pulled Julie to her feet.

"Help, they're after me," Lily cried out, running into Tyson's arms.

"Follow the others and get on the boat. We'll be right behind you," Tyson said, pushing her behind him.

Knives drawn they began to move towards the boat, keeping an eye out in case any of the undead got too close.

"What the hell happened?" Nate yelled.

"I don't fucking know," Drew yelled back. "Luckily, the sand is slowing them down."

"The others are getting in the boat, we should go," Megan said.

Turning, they quickly sprinted to the boat. Sully was standing on the dock, rope in hand, mooring the boat.

"Supplies on board?" Drew asked.

"Yeah, all on."

"Let's go."

The boat sped away just as those things spilled onto the dock.

"Lily, what happened?" Tyson asked, squatting beside the shaking blonde.

"It all went wrong. S–s–so very wrong," Lily stuttered.

"What went wrong?" Kate asked, sitting next to her.

"The experiment."

"What are you talking about?" Tyson asked, stroking her hair.

"The island. We had a few of those zombie things quarantined below ground. A few of us were running tests on them. Somehow, they got out this morning and attacked everyone at breakfast. I hid in the armory and packed a bag of guns before making a run for it. They heard me."

"Are you fucking kidding me? We've been here a year and you kept this from us?" Drew yelled.

"Back off, bro," Tyson warned, putting himself between Lily and Drew.

Drew took a deep breath and looked at Kate. *What the hell were they supposed to do now? How was he going to protect his wife and daughter? Never mind Julie and Maddie.*

"So, what now?" Nathan asked.

"I don't know. How far can we go with the fuel we have?"

"Not far."

"Are there any other islands around here?" Drew asked.

"One—but I don't know anything about it. I don't know what we could be walking into."

"Well, we can't go back to the mainland and we can't just live on this boat. We have to take the chance. Go to the island, a few of us will scout it out while the others remain safely on the boat."

"Okay. We got nothing to lose, right?" Nathan sighed.

Two hours later they arrived at the second island. While the others remained on the boat, Drew, Nathan and Tyson went to scout the land. It wasn't a large island, thankfully. They spent the next several hours ensuring there were no dead creatures or nasty surprises before finally returning to the boat.

"It's all good," Nathan confirmed.

Mooring the boat, they helped everyone to shore.

With their supplies safely stowed under the shelter of a cluster of trees, the men set to work building a camp while Kate checked on Julie.

The sun was just setting as they all settled into their new home. Kate was standing on the beach, arms wrapped around her body, staring out across the darkening ocean.

Walking up behind her, Drew gently wrapped his arms around her. "You okay?"

"It was too good to be true."

"We made it out though, sweetheart."

"This time. What happens when Julie gives birth? We'll have two babies to worry about, never mind Maddie."

"Kate, we're safe for now. We all need to get some rest and work on a plan of action tomorrow."

"I don't want to lose you, Drew. I don't want to lose our daughter, or any of our family. I just want the world to be normal again," Kate cried.

"The world was never normal, sweetheart. There has always been danger in some form or another. Whether it was from illness, weather, terrorists, or just plain bad guys, there was always something terrible around every corner. We just had more going on in our lives that stopped us from focusing on it. We had distractions. We don't have those anymore. But we do have each other, and I would die before I let anything happen to you or to Ellie. I promise you, that no matter what, we will be okay."

"I love you, Drew," Kate said, turning to face him.

"I love you more, Kate," Drew said before claiming her lips with his.

They kissed as if their lives depended on it while the sun set on the horizon, casting a hopeful glow over the young couple. Regardless of what tomorrow may hold for their small group, that moment was the one that mattered, the one that they savored. For what is life without love, but a graveyard of memories.

ABOUT ALEXANDRA REED

Contact Alexandra Reed at authoralexandrareed@gmail.com

Alexandra Reed lives in Cheltenham, UK, and has a day job as a Pensions Administrator. Fascinated with things that go bump in the night, and being a hopeless romantic at heart, Alexandra enjoys creating worlds where light can be seen through the darkness and love wins out in the end.

In her spare time Alexandra enjoys reading, is an advocate for Mental Health Awareness, practices meditation, and has a fondness for hedgehogs, owls, and dogs.

Website: alexandrareedauthor.wordpress.com
Facebook: www.facebook.com/darkandtwistyforever
Twitter: @alexreedauthor
Instagram: @alexandrareedauthor

Printed in Great Britain
by Amazon